From

The Women's Press Ltd
34 Great Sutton Street, London EC1V 0DX

Evelyn Conlon was born in County Monaghan and now lives in Dublin. Her short stories were first published in 1970 and 1971, but for the next ten years she concentrated on poetry. In the early 1980s she returned to prose writing, and her first collection of short stories, *My Head is Opening*, was published in 1987. She is currently working on a second collection. Evelyn Conlon has two children.

Evelyn Conlon

Stars in the Daytime

The Women's Press

First published in Great Britain by The Women's Press Ltd 1990
A member of the Namara Group
34 Great Sutton Street, London EC1V 0DX

First published by Attic Press, Dublin, Eire, 1989

British Library Cataloguing in Publication Data
Conlon, Evelyn
  Stars in the daytime.
  I. Title
  823'.914 [F]

  ISBN 0-7043-4217-0

Typeset by AKM Associates (UK) Ltd, Southall, London
Printed and bound in Great Britain by
Cox and Wyman, Reading, Berks

For Fintan Vallely

Acknowledgments

Thanks to Cathy, Annie and Janet for typing. For other practical help, Tiernan, my sister Teresa, and Clare. For encouragement that was essential as much as it was enjoyable, Nell McCafferty and Pat Murphy. To Bríd Doherty, the schoolteacher who gave me my first faith in the imagination.

The author acknowledges the assistance of The Arts Council/An Chomhairle Ealaíon who awarded her a Bursary in Creative Literature which helped in the completion of this book.

Although the place names in this book refer to real places, the characters are entirely fictional.

Chapter One

'Go out to the street to your father, I hear the horse coming,' Rose's mother shouted at her. It was the cart she could hear. *The Kennedys of Castleross* was not on the radio. It would have been if it had been a week-day. Today was Saturday. In this house they screamed at each other nearly all the time. Only occasionally did mother and daughter speak to each other in normal tones. Rose's father was practically deaf, more so with some people than others, mind you. His deafness, partial deafness, was handy for three reasons. He never heard and so was not part, did not have to be included. Secondly he didn't have to listen. Having to listen to their chat, their arranging of the world, would have eventually driven him mad because he could not, would not understand. Thirdly Rose and her mother could scream at each other without admitting that that's what they were doing. It was only a habit they'd got into because of the father's deafness. The house was run at a high pitch. What did it matter? No one could hear. It was only another eccentricity that would have been remarked upon by strangers if there ever had been any. Presumably his being deaf was not handy in other ways but Rose had not got around to thinking about that yet.

She went out to the street. Sometimes she hated going into the bitter cold, hated not being able to say no, ever, to either her mother or father. She went. Other times she loved going out to the sharp 'Whoa. Whoa there. Whoa. Whoa will you, for God's sake.'

There was always something to be taken out of the cart – a craymery can of skim milk, a bucket of pigs' mail (Rose said

1

creamery and *meal* but didn't mind her father's pronunciation – she hadn't noticed it yet). Then they would take the horse out of the cart. (Rose felt that out was not the right word – the horse was not in the cart, but she didn't mind that either.) Rose was sometimes vague and restless, kicking stones and scuffing the toes of her shoes but mostly she was happy enough with the predictability around her. They would unharness the horse and then she could lead it down to the field to let it loose, winkers over the head, bit out of the mouth carefully, and 'stand well back away from the heels so it doesn't kick you' and then walk back talking to herself.

She was eight and it was the 1950s, it being time, time being judged by the number of days after the birth of a blond white among a darker skinned people, called God, who was to this day stuck up in everybody's house around here. Stuck up was a dynamite word – it could damage a girl forever.

'She's very stuck up.'

'And you'd wonder what for.'

Eight was a hard age to be. She still had not got to be the ten beads of the rosary but at least it was better than being five. She lost interest in the Hail Marys once she got to the number of her years. Up to age eight was nothing. Just the quiet passing away of days to make up a person, the building up of nutrition for important things, the growing taller so you weren't looking dogs and worms in the eye, the storing up of love (the little bit of it that there was) for difficult ages ahead, the learning of manners. She was talking to herself again. Playing the Programme. The Programme, woven together with all the licence of wireless, was Rose's lifeline device. Being an only child and living in a place so isolated that people thought it an exaggeration, the Programme was essential. This game, this reality, was a series of characters that Rose had built around herself with whom she could converse. She changed the line-up every six months, or sooner, if they weren't talking enough to her. Sometimes her aunt Catherine was her mother and Tommy Gaffney her father. Sometimes she had no father. Sometimes she was a complete orphan. She might have one, four or five sisters with names like Caroline, Delores, Lou and . . . one or two brothers. Never more than two brothers because she could not imagine more than two boys, even though between her distant neighbours and her cousins she must have known at least six. Not to talk of the boys at school. Perhaps it was just that she couldn't imagine more than two boys together – they would waste all the Programme fighting. Sometimes she was the best looking of all her sisters just for a change, but usually she was normal looking and very very bright. She discussed the daily happenings and the very rare exciting occurrence as well as the fictional extraordinary events with these characters. All extraordinary events in Rose's head were fictional. The real happenings around her, some of which were in reality bizarre, some cruel, some important, were nothing to Rose, they were just living.

Extraordinary events happened elsewhere and to other people. She related the latest to one or all of her people with breathtaking excitement or with admirable cool depending which humour was in her. She could be a sophisticated child. Sometimes the people in the Programme got on her nerves, she wanted to be alone. She didn't want anyone telling her how to fix her pixie. She didn't want to discuss the daily humiliations of school, the unreasonable behaviour of her mother. Being an only child and living with dispensable fictional characters had its advantages. She could just stop playing. She reached the house.

'Sometimes I wonder how she can dawdle so much. What keeps her?'

'I'm here.'

'Did you close the gate on the horse?'

Of course she closed the gate on the horse. She wouldn't let the horse out into the field and not close the gate. Why would anyone do a stupid thing like that?

'Yes.'

She sat down to dinner. Saturday dinner in the winter was like nice dreams. Hot floury soup, hers was cool enough now because her mother had put it out early to let the boiling warmth of it rise to the ceiling. She soaked the bits at the bottom with the back of her spoon. Lovely soup. It went down to her toes and raced back up her blood again, warming her head. The only soup she didn't like was chicken noodle. In the winter there was nothing to do but have dreams and keep warm. There was less work but it was harder to do because you had to pit yourself against the cold every time you went out the door. Sometimes Rose cried with the bitter cold in her face and in the space between her skirt and the top of her wellies. Her hands were always warm inside the mittens, her ears would sing inside the royal blue pixie. But her face, her face. Sometimes it went solid ivory like a corpse. She'd touched her grandaunt's corpse. It didn't worry her. It wasn't cold in cities. Today they were having stew. She didn't particularly like stew meat but the gravy was like extra special soup and if she mixed the carrots with the potatoes she wouldn't notice them. If her mother was nice enough to give her carrots she could eat slowly knowing that the last bits, potatoes and gravy, would be flawless.

Her father was going to town in the afternoon. Into Ballybay. Into Rock meant going into the village. Into Cootehill. Down to Clones. Down to Monaghan which was north of here. Up to Dublin which was south of here. Down to Belfast which was north of here. Some day she would be going to Belfast on a holiday to her cousins. The school sometimes went on a tour up to Dublin but mostly people went to Dublin to hospital. There was no guarantee that she would get on the school tour when she was old enough to go, or that it would still be to Dublin, nor was she sick in any way, but she would be going to Belfast sometime definitely when she was old enough, her mother had promised. Because her father was going into town she could read her book this afternoon. She would have preferred to go with him but she only got to town for the dentist. She was sent to all the cold dark places with him but never to town. He would have a different voice when he came home. Once she had asked,

'Why's that, Mammy? Why has Daddy a different voice when he comes home?'

Her father had laughed. He had heard her. Her mother tight-lipped had said, 'Now look what you have the child saying.'

Someday she would be able to go to town herself just whenever she liked. Today she would read the Bobbsey Twins when her mother was having a little sleep. The Twins did the most wonderful things, much better than Alice in *Alice in Wonderland*.

Rose's mother slept. Rose read a little. She played two turns on her spinning top but it wasn't as good as it used to be last month. The painted funfair was fading, like the gaudy anticlimactic part of Christmas. She talked a while in the Programme but had no heart for it. She was tired from all the cold so she crept into the bed beside her mother. Her mother was a tall thin woman who had six pregnancies and Rose behind her. The pregnancies, the winter losing of blood that might have been babies (it was always in the winter that she lost) should have made her more grateful for Rose but instead she viewed Rose as some kind of horror when she thought about her. How could Rose have grown, have survived when none of the others did? What was different from the others about her? This skinny, big-eyed child who padded around the place noiselessly, sometimes shuffling she'd swear like an old woman, looking, always looking and saying little. Sometimes she felt that Rose was looking straight into her heart. Because this was the way her mind went when she thought about Rose, she tried not to think too much at all about her. As long as she didn't move her away those few feet that you need for perspective, she could love her as much as she was capable of. She had a menacing feeling that everyone else loved their children more than she loved her one but luckily these things weren't discussed at the time so she could keep it to herself. She liked Rose best when she herself was half waking, half sleeping, like now. She liked the way the small cold body wrapped itself into her back taking an exact body size of heat from her but not hoarding it, rather returning it slowly. Rose liked it too. She could feel her mother's sinewy back through the flannel nightdress passing out

5

the right amount of required heat to her. Warming, warming, warm she drifted into a sleep that was as kisses, as mouths one over the other leaving no space for outsiders. They did indeed fill in some empty places for each other.

They woke together and had hot tea and toast as the darkness fell down in black drifts from the sky eventually covering every patch that had been new blue for a short while that day and grey the rest of the time. They would light the tilley after.

'It needs a new mantle. Get me the mantle. Be sure you don't put your fingers through it, Rose.'

'No, Mammy, I won't.'

She didn't say this with reluctant patience as she might normally be forced to do but rather with secret delight in their dusk communion. It couldn't be better if they'd planned it, this busying about the lamp. Her mother opened the tracing paper packet and took out the white pink-rimmed muslin. She removed the globe carefully as if it was the most precious offering in a rich palace and set it on the oil-clothed table. She placed the mantle on the centre rod, puffed it out enough, pumped up some paraffin and filled the kitchen with a sharp taste that you could swallow and float your head on. Rose could take the tongs from the methylated spirits and clip them exactly inches from the expectant mantle that was waiting to prove itself. She wasn't allowed to smell the meths but she managed always a quick sniff before,

'Don't put that too near your nose.'

Her mother lit the tongs with a match, they flared up, caught the waiting mantle – she pumped vigorously then rhythmically, watching carefully. Rose watched her mother. She saw the new noise, the squeaking of the pump, the spluttering turning into an even hum, the new smell of burning and then there was light.

It was Thursday night that they went to the Haydens' play. Her mother dressed Rose in a skirt and sleeveless jacket that her grandmother had made for her. Her grandmother had called it a costume and had made it from an old dress when they were going to a do in the schoolmaster's house. That was in granny's – naturally she would not be going to a do in the schoolmaster's house here – he was too cross to have a do. The schoolmaster in granny's had a half-door on the house and a long form for people to sit on. Her mother then put a thick cardigan over Rose's costume so that ruined it. No one could see anyway because she also wore her brown coat.

'What's a play, Mammy?'

'It's people on stage.'

'What's a stage?'

'You'll see when you get there.'

She never did see the stage or maybe she did but didn't know what it was and forgot to ask.

Her mother and herself wore their wellies to the bottom of the wee road as far as the big hill because of the potholes.

'Mind the puddles.'

'Yes.'

Her mother carried the bicycle flashlamp. It picked out a circular yellow piece of light which she aimed from eye level down and as long as she and Rose watched the round yellow apparition they could see where they were going. Rose would have loved to carry it because she could dart it up to the sky, and it would create a solid ray of light through the pitch. Her mother knew that this was what she would do so she didn't allow her to have it because she hated the sudden dark flashes before her in the split second it took to drag the yellow beam back from the sky down to the road. Her mother wore a loose check coat that had massive square pockets stuck on the front. There were always mints in the pockets. When they got out to the broad road the dark didn't seem so dark because it wasn't so captured and squeezed together by the hedges. Nearing the village people joined them on their way to the play also. Rose didn't know any of them and would normally have listened all the more attentively for that but tonight she was too pre-occupied with this new venture to pass any remarks on them. This would make for some talking and telling in the Programme.

The play was held in a place called a marquee that wasn't spelt 'markey' so Rose thought of it after as a tent. She'd never seen a tent like this before. She'd only seen the ones made from bags that the Power gypsies lived in. They went to their seats. That year Rose was up to her mother's mid-arm when sitting.

Afterwards she could only shiver terrified every time she thought of the play. There was a blind woman in it and something about a rosary beads. There was also a hunchback. Her mother whispered to her that that was what the man was, even though she hadn't asked. He got his head chopped off. She saw his head rolling over the ground in front of him. The blood dripped down the sword and the headless hunchback stood there, more blood all over where his head had been and a red stalk for his neck. People screamed, Rose was too terrified to let any noise out. She clung to her mother, hot sweat that felt cold running down her back underneath granny's costume. She contracted her body into one rigid piece. It was the only safe thing to do. Her mother never noticed her. She was too busy screaming with the rest of them. Rose never remembered coming home that night. Luckily they were all talking about the thing, on their way out of the tent so they didn't prod her with questions. She would have hated anyone to talk to her because she would have cried. For months after, people – the postman, the creamery man, the district nurse, all the McGoldricks – talked about how well done it was.

'You wouldn't know you were at a play.'

When Rose asked her mother, as she did several times, if his head had really come off her mother answered staccato-like, half-startled, half-worried, 'No. No. How could you have thought that?'

She discussed it in the Programme but they had no answers. Alas, in the end she could go no further than her imagination or at least her imagination could take her no further than what she knew.

Time took the edge of the terror away and let other things intervene. Like Johnny. Johnny was from Artane. He was a small old man, probably forty-five at least. Her mother was forty, she thought, but she wasn't nor wouldn't be old for a long, long time. Mothers tended not to get old, as neighbours did.

'He's not a bad fellow and him from Artane and all.'

This was said not once but over and over again, so that a growing child would not be in danger of not hearing it. She didn't know where Artane was or what it was but it obviously meant bad news. No one good could come from there, unless they triumphed over some monumental dark evil. Rose wondered what evil could be that big. Michael O'Hehir said on a Sunday on the radio, 'The Artane Boys' Band' – but presumably that was a different Artane than Johnny's. Johnny was small and skinny with a thin purplish nose and a dark brown cap. He wore the cap the right way round unless he was milking Williamsons' cows. He worked in Williamsons' for his keep although Rose didn't know that. She thought he was a Williamson from Artane. He turned his cap the wrong way round so he could lay his head against the cow's side when milking, that way he wouldn't hurt her with the peak. He told Rose this once when she went on a message about the horse for mowing to Williamsons'. After that she put him in the Programme for a while as a kind uncle.

Johnny remembered the first day that he saw Rose. He had known that there had been a baby in McGinns' for some years, maybe three, but he'd never seen it on his way past the house. Once he'd seen the shiny paisley curtains jumping frantically against the window in a mock dance – that must have been the child tugging at them from its cot. What was it like to be in a single cot surrounded all the time by people who wanted you and were allowed to have you? His mother wanted him but she wasn't allowed to have him – Johnny believed this fact completely. It was a pity that he didn't have an address because even though he hadn't the money to go anywhere he could have got someone to help him write a letter. Not one of the Williamsons. They were suspicious people and would think that he was trying to leave them. He would have written to her.

To my mother – I do understand your problem. It must have been awful for you. I stayed in the place you left me for a few years. Then I went to Artane. I went to school. Then I was sent to these people when I was sixteen. I work for them pretty hard.

They live in County Monaghan. I look forward to hearing from you.

Your son – Johnny.

PS They always called me Johnny in Artane so I answer to that now.

Funny how little things could put you in mind of big things. Some months after this he was getting water from the spring well. He was filling the tin sweet-can full and emptying it into the two buckets. He didn't put the buckets into the well because the rims of them were caked with dried cows' dung and people used the well for drinking water. He was emptying the last canful into a bucket – his hand, hard as it was, smarting from the thin handle digging into the skin – when he heard a splash and a sudden scream. He whizzed round to see the child knee-deep in the trench that ran alongside the flaxhole. She didn't scream again when he looked at her. She knew that she would be all right. He lifted her out muttering, 'What are you doing here? You nearly put the heart crossways in me.' When he handed her over, a wet stray, at the house there was a stunned silence. Many another house might have sent ranting screams into the air as the mother took out her fear and relief on the child's little legs or backside but not this one. Rose's mother looked in horror at what might have happened. She had got Rose this far nearly to have her drowned a few yards from the house. The child must have sneaked silently past her. For a moment she believed that Rose wanted to show her up – otherwise why would she, her only living child, have done that. And in front of this man who had nothing to do with them, this very respectable family. Rose was content enough not knowing any enormity, certainly not knowing death, and having met that man. The McGinns now had reason to be grateful to Johnny so they began giving him odd bits of work which was how Rose got to know him so well.

'There's Johnny. There's Johnny,' she'd squeal with delight when he would arrive carrying some equipment, a fork, a grape or the back sprayer. In the beginning her mother would tighten. 'No need to make such a display,' she'd almost hiss but over the years she relaxed as she saw how utterly happy Johnny made

Rose and how harmless he was really, considering. Someday, she herself would also be able to make Rose that happy – not today, someday. Rose pottered behind him showing him how the hens laid their eggs, the exact spot where the pigs were born in the sand hole, the place where Daddy had fallen off his bicycle, telling all the time harmless things and also other things that had best been kept inside the family structure. Johnny became a landmark for her, a move from babyhood to something more conscious. If he worked for a day with them she would ask for a week, 'Is Johnny here today?' Then she would stop asking because she could sense some disapproval. She would be grateful when he came again.

When he died she was angry. He would not come again. But then she knew it wasn't his fault (it was in fact partly, because he'd committed suicide) so she felt sad, which was better than feeling annoyed with him. When the adults came back from the catholic funeral – he had been catholic after all, one of their own, even though most people hadn't noticed because he didn't go to mass and was not specifically invited to do so – they sat drinking tea and talking about him. Rose sat in the corner beside the fire.

'I wonder what was his name.'

'I wonder.'

'Hard enough too.'

'The Williamsons will miss him.'

'They will.'

'And no one knew his name.'

They mused and thought about the seriousness of that.

'It was Johnny. It was Johnny,' Rose screamed.

They turned from their solemnity, taken aback, having forgotten that she was there. Her mother was thinking about the inappropriateness of her having known Johnny at all. She could now believe that she disapproved only because he was so obviously unstable. The father was thinking much the same.

'The child's upset,' they said, not half knowing or knowing half of what was moving in her head.

Their attention didn't satisfy her but she pretended it did, because they looked worried and she should enjoy attention like that because it didn't happen every day of the week. Phyllis red the table and the funeral goers went home.

Chapter Two

On her ninth birthday Rose felt big and also happy which was good, because indeed she had her problems. She wasn't popular at school, that was the issue. She knew this. What she didn't know was that no one else was particularly popular either. This was the age when children wanted to be liked but didn't know that they had to like back or maybe like first in order to gain this position. They admired others at the school in a simple way but didn't dwell on the feeling long enough to make it a worthwhile emotion. Rose thought it was only her who was not admired. What might the reason be – could it be her red flannel, which was a rectangular piece of cloth with an uneven carelessly cut hole for her head to go through that her mother put on her every day from October to April? No, because how would anyone know about that? She never used the toilet because of the smell (it made her sick) and the cold wind that blew up through the wooden laths where you hunkered yourself, so no one could have seen it by accident. Could it be her wellingtons or the red rims that were there even when the wellingtons came off in spring or her elastic garters always knotted which she could never keep covered by a neat turn down of the socks? Why should it be any of these, she was not the only person with impediments to dress perfection. Lots of others were even worse, with cardigans, shorter than jumpers, runny noses or woeful, not quite bowl but near, home haircuts. She sometimes thought that it was her lunch. She never had anything but chunks of brown homemade bread and homemade jam, usually plum. Who would ever want to swop with that? Some of the others from the village and even some from beside Aghabog had plain loaf bread. You didn't need anything spread on white bread. Norah Claffey always had sliced bread. White. There was no such thing as sliced brown bread and she sometimes had bananas on it. Sliced white bread with something on it was elevated from lunch to a sandwich. Rose later believed that this was the reason for Norah's extraordinary popularity with boys, although how the boys could have known what she had on her lunch she never figured out. The boys ate their lunches at the other wall. Funny she never wondered what boys had on their bread.

Was it her ribbon? Maybe it was because she had no brothers or sisters, although in this community that should have made her interesting. Or could this be the harbinger, a sign of her future days? Surely not. But it was so bad the best thing for Rose to do was put her head down, small body forward, and plough her way through the major pains of rejection. If only she'd known that Norah Claffey and Una McGaghey felt just as bad.

Sometimes small exciting things happened at school, perhaps parcels of *The African Missionary* or *The Far East* arriving. The teacher would read Pudsey Ryan, taking relish in the bad spelling – what a strange thing for a teacher to do – all the more enjoyable for its strangeness. Every second Friday was library day, you could change your two books and oh the disappointment, the anger at useless slovenly mothers, if you had forgotten the books and had to wait two more weeks to change the books that you had finished in the first three days of last fortnight which was why you forgot them. Sometimes small exciting things – but mostly however school was dangerous. Horrible things were possible. Humiliations. Degradations. Inadequacies and beatings. Beatings hung over the room, they were in every corner, they were hidden in the cracks, they were in the dust that the sun picked out in long shafts, they had slid under the shiny plum paint to become part of the walls. Horrors that were only a minute, a wrong answer, a giggle away from execution. Usually it was someone else's hand. Beatings and hands and canes went together. It would ruin your appreciation of cane furniture forever. It wasn't just your own beating – it was yours multiplied by thirty, so the beating potential in a day was vast. Every time the cane hit bare skin you were reminded that it could be yours. 'Mammy, Daniel got six slaps on the bare hands today.'

'What did he do?'

'Nothing.'

'You don't get slapped for nothing. He must have done something.'

'No, he only giggled.'

'Hand me over that thingamejig.'

The collection of pupils at school was interesting. Their attitudes towards the time spent in the two-storeyed stone building with the plum paint varied, which was not surprising considering the scattered views on education held by the adults whence they came. And the beatings. But Rose couldn't think about beatings all the time – she had already become a person who would try to concentrate on the possible best of things. Some of the pupils never thought about anything else and would in the future head the country with gusto into the depression of the 1980s, their time come at last. There was no unified class structure, as in cities. Everyone went to the same school so far, although no doctor in the village ever had a child so I suppose you couldn't really tell without knowing where it would have been sent to school if it had ever been. But schoolteachers' and farmers' children went, and who else was there? Publicans' and drapers' children went to the school nearest them also. Protestants had a school of their own. They were dull people with money. For some, education was just years up to eleven and then repeat elevens until the child could legally leave. So they relaxed, what the child hadn't learned by Primary it could pick up between eleven and fourteen and if it couldn't then it wasn't meant to. For others education was books and books, any books, were the secret. The way, the truth, and the life. Rose's mother was like that. And Rose sat beside a girl who in thirty years time was to scream at her three year old child, 'Emmanuel, if you don't come here for your dinner this minute I'll send you to school in the morning.'

Emmanuel, starve or be educated.

A temporary teacher came into the school for a week while the real teacher was sick. It was the most exciting thing at school up to then. But on Thursday he had reason to beat Rose. Surely a temporary teacher wouldn't bother. But he did. This didn't help Rose's popularity but something was to happen the very next morning to change things. It was late frosty spring and she was breaking the ice on the bucket with a sharp edged stick. She would then leave the bucket in the hall and her mother would scald the calves' meal when Rose was gone to school. She was pounding the ice, beating in a rhythmic, charmful beat. The idea was to hit it hard enough to crack it but not hard enough to damage the bottom of the bucket. Bang, bang, bang, crack. Crack. There was water oozing past her toes. She had made a hole in the bottom of the bucket. Then a pain came. It gripped her side and took her breath away.

'Mammy, I've made a hole in the bucket.'

Her mother stormed out of the kitchen, down the steps, movement razor sharp cutting through the space that was between her and Rose's ear, the black skirt swinging viciously about her legs, but Rose was saved by the pain. Her face was pinched, sparrow-like and her mouth was open. Rose's mother looked.

'Good God, what's wrong with you?'

The doctor came in his Volkswagen car, rubbed his baldy head and said that it was appendicitis, which they quickly translated into appendix. They got the hackney man to take her to Monaghan hospital. She was in terrible pain in the back of the car. It's a pity it hadn't happened while she was at school. It would have had more impact. It would have made her more interesting than anyone had ever been but hopefully they would hear this evening and they could talk about it tomorrow.

There was the steepest hill that she had ever seen leading to the door of the hospital. The door with its panelled, coloured glass was the biggest she had ever seen, there was also a lift. She would ask later what a lift was. This wonder-piece was to prove

16

inadequate years later for the speedy movement of bodies, live and dead, into and out of the theatre after the Ulster Defence Association had put a bomb in the town. Rose didn't know at nine years of age, nor did anyone else guess, that things like that could ever happen. Rose was not worried about the appendix because once you had got over being born and being a small baby you didn't die for years and years, barring accidents and this wasn't an accident. 'Appendix isn't an accident, Mammy, is it?'

'No, not exactly.'

If it had been serious she would have got going to Dublin. Still, better that it wasn't too serious. She remembered details of how they got her ready – she could hear her mother saying 'They're getting her ready' so she presumed that's what they were doing. Her mother was always right in situations like this. She did not believe that her mother would leave her, but she did. When they had her ready they brought her to a glassy green or enamel green room, gave her an injection, she went to sleep and she woke up. The pain was unbelievable. For three days. She moaned sometimes and silent other patients tip-toed around her, whispering, 'Poor wee child,' coming occasionally to her side and saying, 'Are you all right? You'll be all right. It will get better everyday.' Soothing in the way that women will.

Nurses came and injected her, stuck needles in her bottom and she cried. Bottom was a better word for it. She learned that the smell of methylated spirits meant needles not lamps. Once she turned on her back and pretended she was asleep until the tray on wheels and the smell had gone but the minute she opened her eyes the nurse flew around the corner and jabbed her. The meanie had been spying on her.

On the fourth day she woke to feel contracting stitches and the promise of a general improvement. They had been right. She discovered that she was in a child's cot in the middle of the floor – oh my God. Four proper beds pointed towards her, a woman in each of them. Oh my God. A cot. She hadn't looked before. The pain had been so bad, so cruel, that she hadn't lifted her eyes except in straight up motions only inches from her body. She had to keep the space around her jealously close to herself so that she could fight the scorching cut. How come she hadn't heard the nurse letting down the side when she was giving her the injection? How come she hadn't noticed her mother peering down and into her eyes instead of over into? (Her mother to her surprise had visited her.) Oh well. It was all too late now. She was ruined. And just when she was ruined they moved her to a bed.

But she was grateful to be moved into a bed. She surveyed her other patients. They would have seen her crying. But in the pain she had dreamt that this did not matter and so it came not to matter. There was an old woman with gout in the bed next to her. She was so old that she had nothing left now but superstition. Rose wasn't shocked. She took the hardening (for that's what she preferred to see it as) of the woman's limbs as a fact that warranted no terror. This woman, Sadie, introduced her to fizzy drinks. She had a large many-sided bottle with a contraption on top of it called a syphon and she enjoyed great glee several times a day pouring Rose a glass from this small crossroads pump. Beside Sadie there was a big girl, maybe as old as eighteen or thirty. And two others. And a continuous stream of visitors from other wards. A motley bunch united by some minor or major mechanical difficulty or fault in their bodies.

They burst open teasing views for Rose, because they had conversations. In front of her. Some of them had decided that it would be too difficult to mind their language, others of them felt no duty to shield, to protect her because she wasn't their child, their sister. Sometimes they had throaty laughs (even Sadie) when they talked. It would start with sentences, coming shooting out of them on time in chorus fast as lightning. Then one of them would miss her turn because of the laughing – another would drop out, and another. Then they'd all join in the laugh, one that started way down below their bellybutton, uniting them all in some knowing bodytalk and Rose knew that she was a necessary part of the laugh. The fun was partly in the not allowingness of their talk in front of a child and they might never have got into such a gusto with their conversation if she had not been there, to hide their words from, a child for whom things must be camouflaged. Sadie would sometimes say, 'Shh, the child,' and pour her another glass of fizzy drink.

She remembered this six months later when a visiting priest rubbed himself against her and then gave her a pound.

The patients also talked about body parts she'd never heard of – kidneys, bladders, thighs, lungs, down theres. She saw a bra for the first time – her mother didn't wear one. She saw fat bodies and liked them – they had more presence than skinny ones.

Her mother and father and some of the neighbours visited her. They brought oranges that she couldn't peel, biscuits and one woman brought a Flash bar, which was chocolate around an ordinary slightly softer, penny bar. You had to break penny bars before you could eat them – cup them in your hand at the right tension and hit them in exactly the right spot – the beginning of physics – but Flash bars were softer. You could bite the bit off.

'She's doing well.'

'Yes.'

'She made a great recovery.'

'She'll be out in no time.'

Her father was urgent on these visits. His wife usually handled emotional matters and he was uncomfortable with them.

Her mother came on her own once and asked her questions about the other patients. Everytime Rose tried to tell her about the big girl her mother just said, 'Hmm' and changed the subject or, 'Yeah,' from which Rose deduced that there was something wrong, bad, about the big girl. Also fascinating, because Rose couldn't figure out what could be bad about her. She had a spotless dressing gown and bedroom slippers that were only a wedged sole and a strip of yellow fur. She was also great fun, the person who always lasted the longest in the dropout conversations. Why was she bad?

On the Sunday her mother and father came early and took her downstairs to the Male Medical to visit a man from the next town. They set off from her bed as if going on a major outing.

No one would believe that Rose had only her nightdress on underneath the coat and that she still had twelve stitches in. Rose's mother said politely to the big girl, 'If anyone comes to this bed, we'll be back in five minutes. We're just nipping down to see another patient.'

How sweetly she talked to the bad girl.

They walked down the corridor slowly because Rose was sore. Her father and mother took a hand each, a rare moment of love. It was never to be repeated in Rose's lifetime. Disinfected smells were sometimes overcome totally by disinfectant itself but at other places in the corridor you could smell normal things like fresh air blowing in through the window, like food – soup with white bread, gravy, and vegetables that weren't fried. But the nearer they got to the Male Medical the heavier became the smell until the ward itself surrounded Rose with a total odour akin to fear. Their ward seemed darker too,. There weren't any pinks or flowers or cards or yellow bits of fur. There were newspapers on a few of the beds but no one was reading, no one was talking. Men who saw themselves as boss had to lie on their backs.

They were each dark in their own illness, hating wearing pyjamas, resentful at being looked after by other women, their wives would surely have done it better. The nurses behaved differently here. Those who preferred the capable lives of women made a greater effort at patience, those who were flirts at heart could relax in the less exacting atmosphere of male gratefulness.

Rose's mother did most of the talking to Frank Mackinalley, her father again lost in unfamiliar quicksand. Rose read McNally on his chart. On the way out Frank and he exchanged a few words that didn't amount to much. They walked back to the Female Surgical, all of them relieved. Rose's mother particularly so, because she dreaded to think what it would be like to have a sick husband. Much worse than being sick yourself.

'That's the maternity,' Rose's mother said to Rose's father.

The hospital was like the community itself, not streamlined.

There were nine to nineties here. There was dying and death and the maternity ward but Rose didn't know about maternity yet. She did know about dying but not too worriedly. She was glad to get back to her own ward where being sick didn't mean being dirty. A woman would try for as long as possible not to dribble, no matter how old she was – or so Rose thought. Female sickness was obviously more attractive. Later in life a woman's ward would come as a shock to her – sick women lying, obviously ill if they were being attended, were potentially herself. But today, she was too young to know that this ward also meant dying, not just being sick. Her mother tucked her into bed and watched her restlessly, wishing that Rose were home and they would not have to come to this place to be reminded. But Rose was suffering none of that nervousness in the midst of this great world of overheard excitements. Like any professional patient, she got to know each of the women by her illness and the colour of her dressing gown. One big girl had a silent aura about her ailment, connected in some way with the belly laugh. No one asked about her illness and she didn't volunteer. Rose speculated but came up with nothing more interesting than tonsils or something wrong with her chest. In fact Rose missed a lot going on in that ward but she did learn about the sense of knowing that she was missing something and that was a start.

When she was dressed to go home her mother gave her a box of chocolates to give to the nurses. It was the first time she had ever given a present to anyone. She went into their office, wanting to give it to her favourite nurse, but they all looked the same when bunched together. She couldn't remember which was the sneaky one – she may even have given the chocolates to her. She left then, holding her mother's hand, a wiser girl with a scar and a slight bending over in her body – a protection mechanism against hurting her cut. Some weeks later she straightened herself but only from her pelvis up so she kept a bit of her bottom sticking out, or at least that's what she said in later life when she needed an excuse for her big bottom.

She was treated like royalty on her return home, pink salmon for her tea the first day, floury potatoes in soup for dinner the next. Her head was full of thoughts of people, some of them getting mixed up as the days passed. Her mother said that Sadie was a lovely old girl.

'Why are some women called women and some called girls?'

Her mother repeated the question loudly for her father and they both laughed. Rose asked the question again and they got so embarrassed they were stuck for a minute so they let her ask it again. She enjoyed something in their reaction, their helplessness in the face of her question, but she mistrusted their coyness, their mutual strength solid against her and her doubts. She couldn't figure out what it was but she had a feeling that Sadie and herself did not come out well from the laugh. In time she protected the patients she'd met by not mentioning them. They became active members of her Programme, that way her parents couldn't harm them. In hospital she had been treated as human by others – no one could ever take that away from her. She had been able to say things to them – anything that came into her head, important or otherwise. They didn't disapprove when the first words tumbled out making no sense, they listened, so gradually her sentences fitted together to make some cautious sense. Maybe they had to listen to her, she worried, but they did anyway and so she learned to talk. She went back to school on a real spring morning. They were writing 'Spring Cleaning' at school and pupils were wondering how they could get new-born lambs into the essays or if they should leave that for next week. Material was limited in these sorts of compositions – no one would dare say 'In Italy in Spring . . .'. Rule one was that you kept to what you knew, stayed in your own station, didn't get notions about yourself. Once you learned that, you could survive here or anywhere else, always lesser than you might have been but still surviving. The teacher didn't slap her and made Rose sit when her class had to stand – one half of the school stood as the other used the desks. This treatment suited Rose fine until it came to picking for rounders.

'You can't play. You can't even stand.'

Now she'd be out of rounders for the whole month. Still . . .

Chapter Three

Rose never believed in summer the way adults did. She couldn't believe in what wasn't there, so she missed out on the most important, the 'looking forward to' summer. (The most important part because it was the longest.)

Every year the few weeks of summer would be ending just as Rose was beginning to believe and she would be plunged back again into another winter in danger of developing an 'I told you so' character unless life could do something major to her. And also they wasted the few weeks making hay. Nevertheless summer was good for her, unknown to herself. In the summer she grew up some more, not that she noticed this because of light clothes and freedom of movement. Her arms and legs hung loose so she didn't notice their length increasing as she would have done if she'd had to hold them in around her body for heat or pull down short sleeves around iced wrists, and it was only when she got back into long grey socks, heavy skirts and multiple jumpers that she would notice how much she had extended. Summer always brought other changes. Changes in her idea of herself.

The summer that she was eleven caused particular activity in her. Some days she felt that she was inside herself perfectly – as if she was meant to be. To have been young, to be waiting now for life – life was always ahead – and to get old. Other days she would be outside herself, not knowing what she was here for and feeling itchy or vaguely angry. Up to now if she wondered about the anger, she would have to admit she was angry with God for bringing her here because she hadn't begun to associate her being here with anyone other than God. Only God could have done that. But eleven and a half changed that. It began in little ways, this consciousness. Sometime in May the gypsies in the caravan had a new baby. They always came to the bottom of their road when they were having a baby. That year the midwife came in the middle of the night. She got all the big children, from five upwards, dressed and out on the side of the road but she let the three younger ones sleep on because she hadn't the heart. Also the gypsy woman was fairly well on and in control so she'd hardly waken them. Next morning Rose heard the new baby crying on her way to school and saw Mrs O'Leary sitting in the doorway rocking it. She was staring at her husband who was building a fire in front of the caravan, piling sticks towards the sky. Rose knew then, in the way that knowledge comes inexplicably in flashes to children (indeed also to adults if they let it which they usually don't after twenty-five due to its danger and its unsettling effect) that it was Mrs O'Leary who had the babies, not the whole O'Learys. And if Mrs O'Leary had the babies, then so did all the other missuses. Good lord. Oh my God.

It was a wonderful bit of knowledge but it had incredible repercussions. What was she to do with it? She couldn't just add it to all the other bits of knowledge because it contradicted so many of them. It would sit uncomfortably with naïve notions. No, she was going to have to clean the slate and rebuild. If some of those infallibles were wrong – then how many others? No. It had just been oversight not to know where babies came from. Perhaps lots of girls her age knew. Did any boys know? Unlikely. Aunt Kitty had said the week after Bernadette was born, 'My life was terrible this time. It never stopped morning, noon and night.' Had that anything to do with it? Hardly. That was a bit specific. Now she knew the main part, all would be well. She continued on her way to school, quite happy and unperturbed at having to reassess her whole collection of truths. A tentative sun was testing its own durability on her lanky front. But it gave up and slunk back behind grey black clouds. Rose looked up, noticing the disappeared sun. She wanted to rip the clouds apart to see if it was really behind them and if it wasn't there she wanted to rip the sky apart. It had to be somewhere. How could they be expected to take so much sunlessness?

The summer did come on in fits and starts. It was a long summer in fact – four bright weeks without one drop of rain. Rose nearly forgot about her revelation yet it hung over her in some way – changing things, other things. All things. She would start to play the Programme but then would remember and she would forget about the silly childish Programme that had served her so well.

She had plenty of privacy for marvelling. The house was far enough away from any other house to allow all domestic matters to be truly domestic, never public. No one save her mother, her father and herself had ever seen their clothesline except for the woman who helped with the washing sometimes when her mother was sick. 'Helped or hindered' her mother would mutter which was at least better than the time she had cried and cried when she discovered that the clothes weren't wrung properly and so would never ever dry now. It was the lost baby she was crying for, and herself, as much as the clothes. The house was built on the slightest hint of a hill with a gravel front that was called the street. The garden was a piece of the field that had been there before the house was built and that wasn't needed for the street. It was a desolate-looking piece of greenery that had only three flowers hidden inside it, crocuses and daffodils and daisies. A large hedge hid all this from any unlikely possible passerby.

At night if a stranger were to walk past they would not see the house.

'It's nice to be quiet and private.'

As the house was to the landscape so Rose was in relation to the trio that was called her family. Her mother and father had no access to her mind and she was free to think whatever she liked, to wander around all possibilities without human distraction. She had no one to keep up with, no one to mimic, no model. Her schoolmates stayed present for her while she walked the journey up the road from school but receded every day once she walked over the doorstep. She was indeed alone. And people would have noticed this in chapel where her mother stood beside her alone as every other woman stood with her daughters. What happened their sons they never knew because the boys were on the other side of the chapel and certainly their fathers were not looking after them. And more certainly the mothers did not look over to the men's side. The statues resembled the congregation. There was the strong forthright looking man – face of pride staring down the middle aisle – St Joseph, there was St Anthony making up in tallness for what he lacked in familiarity, and one virgin veiled and demure with a hand only half lifted and that was towards the women's aisle, which wasn't an aisle that mattered.

Rose had learned painfully to stay quiet and still at mass. She'd had the most outrageous things done to her by her mother in this process. She'd been glowered at, clipped on the ear and even nipped. In the end these travesties of decent behaviour worked, Rose was shaped into docile subservience. No matter how the wood dug into her knees nor how she thought that mass would never end she wore the mask that every decent female catholic took upon themselves supposedly willingly. Because she wanted to be part of them all. She wanted to be perfect. Here, the vicious and mean donned servile looks of piety that could fool anyone even themselves, unless a person had had a moral run-in with them and had seen their charity then for what it really was – a thin disguise of fear and tight hatred. When the priest turned to the people and said '*Ite, Missa Est* – Go, the Mass is ended', there was a general relief which the feigning pious tried not to show. They teemed out of the chapel then, saluting neighbours and talking to visitors home from Dublin, England or America. Sometimes mothers called over escaping children (more so girls than boys because they were nearer and perhaps because the mothers were a little afraid of what their sons might think) to be looked at by some amazed visitor who just couldn't believe that so and so had got so big.

'And isn't she the image of Paćkey?'

Years later this showing of offspring would be repeated by more mothers (these same young girls twenty years hence) who would either have forgotten their own rage, embarrassment, bewilderment or else decided that a child's emotions were less important than its mother's. The time would also come when mothers who weren't married could do this too with their children, but that time was not there in Rose's eleven-year lifetime. Rose didn't connect the facts with these goings on but they were intrinsically linked (and she would learn that also someday). This showing of young girl, child, to classmate of twenty years ago was an important part of the encouragement to people the world. The young girls would without doubt be the mothers and grandmothers of countless children that were at this time not even possible dust specks floating in the universe. These unborn children were only certain because women had always done it and there was no reason to believe that they would stop now.

Mass in her grandmother's was different. The people were bigger – big men with redder faces than at home, big women with more children apiece. There were cushions on the kneeling part of the seats.

Her grandmother had been born in 1896. Nine of her brothers and sisters lived. She had worked for some time as a priest's housekeeper – scrubbing cement floors with cold water at six o'clock in the morning. She would have preferred to scrub floors of her own and in time she did. She married Rose's grandfather when she was still young, not because she was modern but because that's what they did in that decade.

Her grandmother was delighted to get away from the priest's house. She then used her life, her body, her soul to have over one dozen children and over forty-five grandchildren and an as yet undecided number of great grandchildren to pass on her smile to, lucky individuals who would never think, when being complimented by rank strangers in the four corners of the earth, where they had got that particular smile; with unwarranted vanity they would think that it had started with them. She moved with ease through her role, partly through ignorance, partly from exhaustion. She did her best with her life. At her funeral the chapel would be packed with children and grand-children, some of them the spitting image of her. One descendant would notice this common thread, would say nothing for fear of being judged sentimental. Rose spent a holiday with her grandmother every summer and learned her own importance there.

Granny's children were mostly reared, the youngest was twelve so she had time to walk, to visit. Rose walked with her grandmother to places miles away past the well. They crossed fields, the shortcut, to visit people, nearly up to their necks in muck. They checked the ducks, the geese and their laryngitic ganders on their way. One house had no laneway into it no matter how you approached it.

Two houses were of particular interest to Rose, one with an adopted child, who had a different status to dead Johnny, and another where her grandmother said a man lived who had the quare notion of your mother, her oldest child. Rose wouldn't have believed this yet, even if she'd known what a notion meant. But she was interested because her grandmother said this with her conspiratorial grin on her face.

'Get me the thingamejig.'

Rose would go to the old house and say,

'What might the thingamejig be?'

Then granny would get cross with Rose because she didn't get it. This thingamejig might be the twig brush or the hens' eggs or then again it might be anything. Once she saw her grandmother trying to force poison down a dog's throat – the other side of a woman whose heart was beaten out of her with winter's exhaustion and work. Rose tried to forget it because if she didn't she would have to hate granny for the rest of her life. After all they drowned pups at home too and all she did was wrap her arms around Lassie's throat and cry with her, rubbing her all the time and telling her that it would be all right in the morning. Typical panacea for uncomfortable wrong deeds.

Rose overheard her grandmother talking to a neighbour.

'There she was talking away to herself at the corner of the

house. Playing I suppose, I thought there was a half a dozen on the street.'

This was a complete breach of confidence. She'd have to forget that as well. She must take the bad with the good. Her grandmother had a language of her own – she talked chimmies and shifts, drawers, and spoke of grown-ups as if they were no better, no wiser than Rose herself. She brought Rose, who now knew what a stage was, to a variety concert. A tall man with a black suit, a white shirt and dickey bow told lots of jokes about women. Rose supposed that to be good for women but her grandmother didn't appear to agree. She said to Mrs Reilly on the way home, 'And did you see his wife after? Who would have thought she'd be so fine looking?' It was her way of taking him down a peg or two, a sort of contorted revenge on him.

The other fascination with granny's was that there were aunts and uncles at weekends, home from various places. There was lots of shaving and bustle on a Sunday night as they got ready for dances. There was make-up and teasing and the writing of love letters of which she was only slightly aware. But the best of all was granny. In the real world it may not have mattered what women said or thought. It may not have mattered what they felt. They may have been the guardian of only the emotional but Rose didn't know that when she was with granny. In fact she believed that women like her granny decided everything between them. In reality her grandmother belonged to a mass of Irish women who had not one choice available to them about anything in their lives except perhaps the naming of their children, and that after consideration had been taken of everyone else's wishes. Their grandmothers before them had starved in the famine, their mothers had been thankful for minor improvements after that, all the time they all had become and became pregnant without choice. Choice and babies couldn't go together. Choice and marriage were natural enemies. No one had ever heard about an orgasm, not even men and they had them. Words like choice and orgasm, particularly choice, were futuristic and had no place in this poverty-stricken cauldron, although ideas did hit the odd woman maybe five times a lifetime but naturally had to be abandoned.

But Rose wouldn't know that for some years to come.

Rose never made connections between her grandmother and her mother until that summer, because not until then did she realise that what she was dealing with in her grandmother's were womanly matters. Some wet Sunday after that particular holiday Rose was looking at the photos in her mother's photo album and also at the ones which seemed as if they'd spilled from the album into a shoebox. She pored over past fragments –

'What's your name, Mammy?'

'You know my name. Phyllis.'

'Phyllis.'

She rolled it around her tongue as if she'd never heard it before. Rose's mother in that moment became a Phyllis, a real Phyllis because Rose was eleven and a half and it was summer. Rose knew things this summer that she hadn't known last year and Phyllis suited the gangly photo in front of her at that minute. Phyllis. Phyllis, the mother of Rose, the daughter of granny. Phyllis. I see. Things were falling into place, a place outside of innocence which once reached could never be swapped for a simpler view. Her mother's wedding photo was sparse, the costume was buttoned from neck to waist, the pleats were sharp as knives, the wedding pair held hands bent from the elbow making their arms into formal L-shapes. Only a hint of a smile passed momentarily over their faces. There was a war on – which was also why her mother's wedding ring was narrow. Her grandmother's wedding photo was more casual, the dress was longer than the coat, a scarf was slung around her neck and she leaned on the groom positively grinning, one hand on his shoulder as he stood there casually, amused by this woman who was now his wife. He might have looked at a loss to know what to do next, except that he had a handlebar moustache and for Rose any man who had the nerve to grow hair on his face knew what he was doing. He looked a good man and indeed turned out to be that despite what one might think when counting the children in ten years' time. Men were divided into good and bad – a really good man was someone who came from the fields worried every month and enquired kindly if she was all right. A good man was one who an odd time realised that the year was divided into months, not just farming seasons and who cared, even if he never said it. A bad man was hard to define because he came in all forms and for different reasons. Around these parts the men were mostly fair to middling good.

Half a century later they would say there weren't many batterers among them and you could believe them if you wanted to because they certainly didn't look like batterers or you could wonder, because someone somewhere had to make up the numbers and surely this place was no more innocent than others.

Yes, the wedding photos were different. Rose looked at her father out of the photo, sitting today in the corner backed by emulsion paint. Surely that man had not proposed to her mother. Granny and Granda maybe – look at them – but never her father and Phyllis. Still she was going to have to get these facts right. Her grandmother had had her mother and her mother – mind you that was another day's thinking. She was reluctant to pursue it or say anything. She didn't want to owe anything. Phyllis herself had known reluctances like these. She had given birth to Rose into a time when daughters kept their secrets if they had any.

The only thing that Phyllis and her mother had ever said to each other over the years was an occasional, 'It's hard going all the same.' They never even commented on Phyllis' one to her mother's dozen. The less said the easier mended. The less thought the easier the hard going would be. Four weeks after Rose had been born, luckily, Phyllis' father had got ill so she had to go home to help. The feeling of being home – really home. Married women should not admit that home was home. Phyllis found it easier here with the baby. In her own house she had been panicked at moments or else a heaviness had sat on her head and hung over her eyes threatening to make her blind with crying forever. She had been unable to cope. With only one child. She would never be able to admit that. Here at home a system had been set up, the history of these domestic matters had been declared. There was a system to the washing, the drying, the airing of clothes, the cleaning of house and people. There were basins for different things. The cycle of warmth and air had been going through the house for forty years now. It was easy to keep things going because it would have been harder not to. The very air would have rebelled. Yes, it was nice to be home but Phyllis said nothing. A small reluctance.

In time Phyllis had got used to the baby, helped by the fact that she and her husband worked side by side. She was not alone in black loneliness like the women in futuristic dormitories. She put his dinner in and out of the oven when he had to leave the table to check that the horse in the cart hadn't turned it over. He said nothing about this perfect caring but still he was not a bad man. The standards of bad and good for men were tightening up – a little, just a little, not half as tight as they were going to get. Phyllis' husband did well on the scale.

Now the baby was peering at photos, asking questions. Peering at her, Phyllis, in pictures of the always better past. The future was no land, the present unacceptable, the past always better. The child still squinted at the pictures, judging her harshly she was sure, which wasn't, in fact, true.

Chapter Four

A more confident Rose prepared to go back to school that autumn, cheered by the fitting together of connections she had achieved over the summer. It was unfortunate, considering her goodwill towards her granny and her mother (now Phyllis) that at this same time she became aggravated by some of her mother's more obvious habits.

She began to detest the whispering of prayers at mass. The mutter, always out of beat with some other woman's mutter mutter, left Rose rigid with temper. The rosary beads rattling through hands, each bead falling gratefully towards the downward apex as her mother sent up another supplication. There was worse to come, but for the moment Rose boiled up only about issues of prayer. The preparing for mass.

'Have you got your beads?'

She would step into her parents' room for the beads where they hung like immovable nooses on the dressing table mirror. The mirror tilted itself defiantly into the room, despite the ugly piece of furniture that it adorned, and it helped a little by this gesture to brighten the room. The removal of the beads gave it a clearer view. Rose could see herself. A hatred flashing. What on earth for? She would try not to let her emotions get out of hand. Because things were good enough to compensate for these and other growing pains. She looked at her classmates in front of her at mass and for the first time looked forward to going back to school. She particularly looked at the back of Rosaleen Connolly's head, bringing her down to size as good as any east wind, by her unsuspected stare. Never again would she let that girl humiliate her.

'Can I play with yous today?'

And Rosaleen Connolly would say no, thus forcing her to play with no one for that day and maybe every day of that week. Boys at least hit each other. On Tuesday,

'Can I play with yous?'

'Rosaleen Connolly says no.'

No power was ever so complete as can I play with you power or rather no you can't power. Never again. She was determined. Indeed doesn't confidence come with the summer.

The reason for this enthusiasm was that Rose was having an unknown experience called a notion. She would have been having crushes if she had come from somewhere else or from some future time. Notions were what they had around here. She thought that she was just happy. Very happy. People were nice, particularly boys, even boys at school, particularly one boy. And she was going back to school next week.

Over the next six months her love grew to astonishing proportions – for that was what it was. What had started as a mote underneath her heart soon filled the whole of her body to bursting point. By now she knew that it was love and carried it with her well, considering the shock she had got when she first realised. He was fair, delicate and soft spoken. He had a fringe. He was divine. It could all become sinful if she thought about it too much. She would learn to ration the thoughts of him and maybe, please God, it would only be a venial sin.

She cycled to the village early one morning on a message that had to be done before school. It was a privilege to be out at that hour of not yet begun day. She descended the hill freewheeling. The blue smoke was wending its way upwards from the early risers' houses, merging in some places with the lifting mist. All movement except hers was skyward. Gilliland's dog plodded across the street, slightly curious about the bicycle at wakening time. But he changed his mind about this minor interest and flopped down, blinking, in the middle of the road, confident that there would be no traffic for a long while. Only someone outside on a bicycle or on foot could imagine the lives in each house at this hour. The people inside were too busy living them. Rose was a person outside on a bicycle. She ticked off the kitchen scenes in every home with precise simplification and, it must be said, a lot of correctness. She was coming to his house. She back-pedalled to delay the moment, same way as the adults did with summer. Even though she could not look forward to summer, she had at least got the message. She would be at his door soon and then because it takes such a short time to pass a door it would be over until her way back. What if he looked out? Would their eyes sink into each other, but no that couldn't happen because he would be too busy right now. She fancied that he was at this moment helping his mother with the small children. He would be a wonderful person in the mornings, as always. She wasn't actually sure if there were smaller children in the house. In real fact he was at the moment sulking furiously in a corner after getting a clip on the ear because he had tried to steal one of his sisters' pieces of lunch for himself. The indignity of people is of course always themselves.

Rose was now past his door and made her way up the hill revitalised by the sudden shock to her heart that had come when her bicycle was perfectly parallel to his door. On another morning, before love, she might have noticed details of the village but today she did her message and got back on her bicycle full to the crown of her head with honest emotion as she waited to repeat the perfect experience. It was over, she was cycling out the far end of the village on her way from where people had next door neighbours, lived in houses with toilets and water and shared a street with him.

Over so quick. She had picked sticks for school with him when they were younger and she had not realised, but now that she was – well, in love – they would never put the two of them together. It was impossible. Still, she could see him every day. She doubly hated sewing and knitting now. Before this she had hated it because she could not keep any of her specimens clean, she didn't know the difference between nor even the names of longways and angleways stitches, her knitted toes looked like knitted heels, the teacher hit her knuckles with a ruler. Now it also kept her out of the same room as him for an hour on a Friday. The girls had to do sewing and knitting with the mistress, the boys could stay with the master and do nothing. On a Friday with time running out before the weekend. Still she'd get a good face-on look at him on her way back. Rose was becoming an optimist. Someday she would kiss him. She was getting brave. (Indeed she was to kiss him more than a decade later, beside the fire of a watchman's hut in a city, and it was to be even then, despite the dawning brutalisation of life – and the book – a kiss of complete innocence, a surprised flutter of wonder touching their lips.)

Phyllis did a big washing on a Monday like every other woman before and since. She did it both inside in the kitchen and if it was a dry day, outside on the street. The whites boiled on the range, the very dirty steeped outside, the stuff that was ready was in the tin bath sitting on two chairs. Her instruments were a washboard and a bar of Lifebuoy. She rubbed each garment against the board until it was spotless, making her fingers and knuckles raw red. When she was pregnant she tried to raise the bath or to sit down while she scrubbed, in order to save her back. It never even saved a baby, except for Rose. She tried to keep water from splashing on the cement floor or else she would have to wash the floor as well. Rose's heart dropped when she saw the bath but there was cabbage mixed with potatoes fried on the pan for dinner. Butter, salt and milk. By the time she had eaten she was resigned to washing day.

Phyllis looked like a woman reluctantly about to impart a secret. She blurted before she changed her mind, 'I'll give you one of Annie MP Smithson's books to read.'

Mrs McQuaid had told her that they were handy books for a growing girl. They were indeed because by long sentimental graft they told how unnatural the immoral was, how immoral the unnatural. Girls became women. Women were mothers, spinsters or widows. Mothers loved their children. Phyllis, who had read them all herself, *Travellers Joy, The Walk of a Queen, Nurse Harding, The Light of Other Days*, wasn't totally sure of their suitability. There were innuendos. A child would have to ask why Nora was keeping her pregnancy secret for as long as possible, why her pregnancy was welcomed when her family learned that she had been secretly married. A child might ask, but how could she have been pregnant if she wasn't married. Or at least a child like Rose might ask. But Phyllis did agree with Mrs McQuaid that they were very very sad so she supposed that was as good a help to any growing girl as she could get. (Some decades later Rose would return the compliment, if that's what it was, buying a set for Phyllis from the sort of man Anne MP Smithson would have approved of herself.) Anyway, Mrs McQuaid knew better because she had more children. She said that the next five years would be important.

And so Rose was brought further into a woman's terrible world where romance was all she could ask for and marrying was all she could get. She went to the mobile library every fortnight, up the two steps that the librarian ceremoniously put to the open door, and exchanged now two navy hardbacks for two more navy hardbacks. Choosing the titles was nearly the best part. Sometimes as she looked through adult fiction for another Annie MP she felt a hankering after the children's section – *The Secret Garden*, where evil could be reformed and the orchard meant more in the end anyway, but it was a hankering that she felt could not be indulged. Phyllis would surely be disappointed if she came home with a child's adventure. The same hankering sometimes came on her for the Programme and when it did she lapsed without any hesitation, only blushing slightly at the end when she felt that this sort of child's world was really inappropriate to a grown girl.

These days in the Programme she always had a brother. Other times in previous years a brother had died tragically and she had helped to carry his coffin to the shock of all the village. But now he was here again large as life because he was useful due to the fact that he had friends. She flirted in front of his friends with dignity and seriousness, of course. She was a confident individual when their world was too much for them, as it often was. She spoke rarely but when she did they all turned to look at her. They tried not to notice how lovely she was because they wanted to listen to what she was saying. Annie MP was indeed working, yet Rose was a little ashamed of these outings into her imaginations. They didn't seem as constructive as before. In fact the dignity bit seemed disgusting, not at all the stuff for an only independent child.

Tannagh Sports came. Rose had run and won races before but she did not want to this year. She wanted to walk around the field the whole day if necessary to see him. He wasn't there. She met her uncle instead. Last year she would have said to him, 'That tickles, do it again.' Now she talked to him from five feet away in a tone of voice that made her uncle blush and hope he hadn't kept up the teasing for too long. He asked her if she was racing and she said no, disdainfully. The idea of her running exposed down a field towards those parents of little sense who were cajoling their children and those that were more reserved like her mother saying nothing! All this was repugnant now. Her uncle understood what was behind the disdain. Somehow Rose's calm was getting out of her grasp. Her Programme, her imagination was all wrong. It was undignified, but where was she to hide herself and her new desire?

With the new feeling came sometimes a gnawing sense of boredom. On her way home from school she would occasionally think, perhaps there will be an emergency. Maybe a calf dead – that would bring someone to the house. But there would be nothing but Annie MP. A cow stuck in the shuck. That would bring lots of people, lots of shouting and rope and pulling and congratulations.

One Thursday this did happen – a cow in the flax hole.

'Go to McGivern's for another rope. Quick.'

She flew on the bicycle. Her socks dropped to her ankles and the oil of the chain made greasy marks on her bare legs. They said afterwards that she had done it in jig time but it was too late. When she came back the men were on their final heave, shouting at each other, frantic in their pulling, trying with fury to save livelihood from the elements. This time they failed. They got the cow out and dripped poteen into her mouth but she lay lifeless, a mound bigger than themselves reminding them that even leaving their own deaths aside they still would not always win. They talked it over in the kitchen, her father whispering a little, then raising his voice as he realised that there were still men there. Rose shivered and felt sorry for the cow, trying not to think that she had wished it. She shivered again – she had willed not just wished it. It was her fault but they would never know. She could hide it in the same places she hid her desires – in a watery place outside consciousness and so away from choice or guilt.

Rose and her mother and her deaf, partially deaf, father were what was called around those parts comfortable enough. Viewed from any other place with even a modicum of wealth, they were poor. They didn't have some things like a phone, a tarred road, television, electricity, an inside toilet, milk bottles, running water, carpets, milk bottle tops, any electric things which meant a washing machine, flowers (except daffodils and crocuses and daisies that just grew), a car, a tractor, an Aladdin lamp or soup spoons. They did have an outside toilet that never let in water, some fresh vegetables, eggs (two decades later known as a speciality called free range), an open fire in the big bedroom, and modest needs. They also had gutters, 'It's the gutters that gets to a body at this time of year.' 'You're right there missus.' Rose had something else as well now. She had her love for him.

This compensated for a lot of the things they didn't have and gave her a silent glow of her own. It also brought a dilemma with it – should she now be ashamed of what they had not got? She'd heard the fuss when aunts and uncles were getting married. The woman who was going to be the bride, in tears to her sister, 'Look at the state of this house.' An uncle to be a groom, 'Well I can't bring her here with the place looking like this.' And grandmother always cool, 'Well, we'll do our best. That's all we can do.' Rose looked over the fields in the direction of his house – there was one spot from where she could actually see the tall chimney at the back of his home but standing gawking at it would surely bring notice and maybe worse – and pondered over whether to be ashamed or not. With alarming consequences (and it was alarming in a time when children were expected not just to have but to be made up of complexes, their lives meant to be a fight against their total inadequacy and if that wasn't the case then they were too big for their boots and would never come to any good) she decided to be happy with what she'd got and not got. Not to be so was too big. There were too many things involved. She couldn't dig a hole to make a well – although the spring on the very street was worth a dream or two. She couldn't tar the road or make the men fill the potholes by wishing, so she rearranged the emotions that she was meant to have and ended up satisfied. She never let on. If they could have seen inside her head they would have been alarmed at other things too, in particular one other rather large thing, that might lead to more dangerous doubts.

It started – the feeling – with her not having milk bottle tops to buy black babies with. Farmers' children brought money instead to school but it was not as romantic as milk bottle tops. The master distributed *The Far East* and *The African Missionary*. They prayed for the missionaries and they bought black babies. She wished she had milk tops and in the thinking of it she got uneasy about the buying business. What if the baby didn't want to be bought, what if it wanted to stay as it was? What if its mother didn't want it to be bought or to sell it? A small doubt was growing about good and evil, the missions and the master. Nerve, Rose. Nerve. The doubt will keep. Nerve. She was white, poor, Irish and a girl from the country and an only child getting wise. The only thing she didn't know was that she was white and that white men were bullies. Nerve, Rose. Nerve.

The months went on. All was more bearable, even the mutter mutter – the tolerance of people in love. Because he was in the chapel too, as well as in the school. He would go to communion on the first Sunday of every month. She would be sure to go first. She would walk up, take the host on her tongue, careful not to commit sacrilege by letting it touch her teeth, turn to face the congregation – was he looking at her – and piously go back to her seat. She would pray fervently for forgiveness for her dreadful sins, hope not to burn in hell forever and then, with the true catholic capacity for self deception, collapse into bad thoughts as she prepared herself to watch him. She kept the praying pose up – her head in her hands, but she raised head and hands up from where they had been dramatically flung on the back of the seat in front of her, and placed her elbows, instead of her forehead, on the back of the seat in front of her. Then she parted all her fingers slightly. If she parted two of them widely enough to let vision in it might be noticeable so she parted them all slightly. This reverent child stayed in that position until he was well and truly gone to the back of the chapel. Then she sat up to hear the announcements so satisfied, so pleased, so happy.

She could never be like Margaret McEnroe, Mena McGold-rick, Maisie Wynne all from the village. She'd seen Mena and Maisie last week in the post office. They were bigger than her and passing eleven affected different girls in different ways. They had outgrown their childish gigglings and the jokes of last year that they still didn't understand, but they clung to the juvenile shoutings of unloved children who must squeal to get notice.

'Mena, do I get him to put the stamp on for me?'

(The same Maisie could and did put five children to bed in ten minutes.) The two girls giggled frantically.

'Maisie, have you got the money for the stamps?'

False false laughter. They twisted and turned, did everything but throw themselves on the ground screaming what is wrong with me. Despairingly they floundered in early adulthood not knowing what to do about anything, particularly their lost interest in each other. Because that lost interest was frightening – if they were fooling each other then surely they could fool themselves but on the brighter side so could they fool everybody else, including the man behind the post office counter. Who had originally come from Doohamelt.

'Mena, where's Doohamelt?'

'Beside Aughnamullen, you plopsty-faced eejit.'

The man smiled, encouraging them. Oh it was sad. Yet Rose envied them their vulgarity, their bravery, even though she felt safer with her own quietness. They left the post office not speaking to her, barely passing their eyes over her because she was only from outside the village. No, she could never be like them.

The following week after school there was a circle around what she presumed was two boys fighting. She had been kept in so it could have been there a while. It didn't sound like boys fighting because you could usually hear the smacks of their fists on each other's faces as they committed traumas on the flesh of each of their mothers. And there were no girls screaming. Girls usually screamed during fights because of an inherent civilisation, black fear, and haughtiness. Boys laughed at the girls screaming and encouraged whichever fighter they were betting on with all the gusto of the cruel men that they would become, unless they were civilised by one of the screaming girls. She daundered over to the circle and made her way to the front through a gap that was being left by a retreating flushed boy. She saw before her the strangest thing. One of the big boys had one of the big girls pinned up against the wall and was trying to kiss her at minute intervals. She screamed every time he tried to kiss but seemed content enough otherwise to stand pinned to the wall by him. There would be a silence, she would look towards Couslas field, he up Coravaccan Lane, then he would try to kiss her again. She would scream. He would stop trying, then they would resume their tranced positions. The crowd was silent. Rose stared, something like a pain that wasn't a pain thumping at the top of her legs. She never knew how long she stood there transfixed, looking at this secret, knowing that there was something wrong and something right about it.

'The master's coming.'

They scattered like stung bees and Rose walked home, just not sure.

The next day her real friend Barry – red-faced, dirty-hands Barry – leaned over her desk and said in the fashion and with the nerve of a man negotiating a fair deal, 'I was told to ask you to come to the wood tomorrow. We're putting on a play.'

Rose had never been asked by any of them ever before. She

didn't pass out although some blood did rush down her. She said quick as a flash. 'I'll ask.'

'I was told to tell you anyway,' Barry said, blown up with importance at having delivered the message right.

'All right. I'll ask.'

How would she ask? How could she phrase this? Would she talk about the play they'd seen in the tent? Would they believe her? Would they let her? My God, will he be there?

Phyllis said no. No. No. And that's that. Rose knew that the emphasis had something to do with the big girl and the big boy yesterday. She just knew it. News had wings around here. Rose vowed to hate her mother until the day she died and after. She didn't tell Barry that she couldn't go. She just didn't go. All this time *he* had never spoken to her. But after she didn't go to the wood, he started to look straight at her. Rose didn't know what to do. It was uncomfortable. He was ruining it. One day he shook his fist at her. She was puzzled. He was destroying it all little bit by little bit.

Towards the end of that puzzling month, she was walking down the stairs. He was behind her. When she came to the turn he bumped into her, made a lunge at her chest, stuffed a shiny book into her hand and ran past her. The book was folded in four – she pushed it under her skirt band and walked on as if nothing had happened, holding herself like a man's whistle, until she could get over the hill where no one could see her. She took the book from where it had met reverently with her skin and looked at it curiously. She sat down on the ditch. It was a peculiar book. There were pictures of Elvis Presley whom she had heard of, and other film stars that she heard people at school talking about. Mostly women. They all had huge huge . . . they were sticking out all over the book. The women had half-open lips, trance expressions – there was that look again. It was indeed in fashion. Most of the women had blonde hair. They had big dreamy eyes. She thought that there was something rather sad about them. She didn't notice the men in the book although it was nice to know what Elvis Presley looked like – would she remember that was him if she saw him again? Why had he given her this? What possible motivation? Could it be that he wanted her to pick out a favourite film star so she wouldn't be so ignorant among the other girls? Could it be that he wanted to involve her in big notions? Could it be that he was being nice? She smarted. He wasn't being nice – he wasn't thinking of her at all. There was something wrong. She knew it. It never struck her that she had a lesser body than the women in the book or that perhaps that was what he was trying to tell her. In her own way she was either too young or too unreasonably confident. Rose folded the book in four with the resolution of bitterly disappointed generations behind her, and put it back under her skirt. She hid it in her room that night, not once tempted to look at it while the paraffin lamp was still lit. She put it beside her skin next morning and went to school.

She could have been terrified about giving it back to him, could have been sorely disappointed that her first chance of talking to him was not going to happen, she could have been angry. Instead she became a solid concept, she became her own resolution to hand back his book without saying one word, without looking at him. She managed this and the way she did with a stoicism that was even more than disdain, gave her pride. One wounded Rose. One proud Rose. She never spoke to him again – not for over a decade. And then she didn't mention it.

In the following few months she let the hurt sink into one central point then let it radiate out slowly. When it came back to the surface she knew more about the emotional inadequacy of boys but she wasn't aware that that was what she knew. She thought she was only just hurt. She could have moved in a number of directions then. Strangely, she chose the path of multiple notions of the male rather than a state of non-notion or a switch in love from him to another boy or a development of the notion of girls. (Thank God for that anyway.) What did these loads of notions mean – were they perhaps the whispering of a promiscuous woman to be or were they a survival mechanism based on the idea that the more spread the less possibility of hurt? And who were these notions of? Her cousin Barney, who was two years older than her, the postman who was fifty years older than her, Brian who was the same age, a Martin who was a vague relation and could have been a year younger than her, and her father's best friend who was aged around fifty. Among others. Why did she spend such time on these electric flashes that ran like falling dominoes along her nerves? It wasn't just that there was nothing else to do. What did these notions mean to her? They meant that she always had a something to brighten every day – whether at dropping potatoes, picking potatoes, taking the horse to have it shod, going to mass, or to school. Notions were like, or else were, long stretches of a feeling of well-being. There was always someone to think about, there was always someone's lane or house to pass or townland to pass through. It was really in a sense the Programme with extras. Sometimes she disliked the new thoughts intensely, screwing her face as if she had sucked lemon, and resolving to go back to the time when she never had any notion of anyone. But it turned out to be an impossible retracing of time.

Rose was coming to the end of her country schooldays. Town would be next with one year in seventh class. The Primary exam had turned out to be such an easy test that she didn't do extremely well in it because she was puzzled, thinking there was a trick somewhere. On the day that she was leaving she felt big, important and terribly excited. She eyed the cane. She could match hairline marks on her hand with the pattern of it – particularly with the pattern on the broken part. And there were other hurts attached to it that went inside her so deep they would not surface for years. She tried by staring at it, to take back to herself some of her world that had been beaten out of her. She watched the parts of the room that she liked – the doors of the library cupboard. It was indeed a perverse achievement that books, the learning of which was associated with assault and being slapped, could be of such love to her. The master did not refer to the fact that her or anyone else's primary education was over that day. All that week sixth class left in dribs and drabs, except for those who would stay another year, and who knew how big was their degradation?

She went down the stairs, beating back a nausea that came on with relief. She said goodbye to three people. Two boys jumped over the wall, and it was over. But then a terrible thing happened. Her mother and father said that she wasn't meant to leave until the next day so they sent her back in the morning.

She actually thought of not going, of hiding all day in McGeough's field but it was only a thought. She walked down the road into the school yard heavy with shame. She even bet to herself that she would get slapped today. She was a big girl who'd had the bigness taken away from her for another day. What a fool they would think she was. How they would glory in her humiliation. In fact nothing like that happened at all. They never really noticed – they had either forgotten that she was supposed to have left or they had forgotten her because she was left. That day – a Friday in the nineteen hundred and early sixties – she did quietly leave national school forever.

Chapter Five

One year and two months later Rose became the luckiest girl in the whole wide uneven world, she got to secondary school. Allowed to go. Got to go. Was able to go.

It was like having a baby really. She was the first. Rose treated the other pupils the way a woman in a maternity ward talks to other first-time mothers – sceptically – because she knows. She thinks – knows – that she is the only one who has done it.

In between there had been that humiliating scholarship year best forgotten about. It was like this – if she didn't get a scholarship she was doomed to commercial class, repeating the same year four times over until she was old enough to get a job. If she did get a scholarship she would get to secondary school and could be anything, even a teacher. How to work up the necessary panic at the prospect of commercial class and so make herself work harder yet how to keep that horror somehow controlled in case, in case. How to dream of a secondary school where you had 'subjects', things like French, and Latin and Science as well as different teachers for every class, without crying because she might never get there. *They* would get there anyway because they had money, why couldn't they only let poor people, like her, do the scholarship? Maybe she would get it anyway. Maybe an office job would be all right after all, but she didn't think so. Yet who was she to think of French and Science? An office job and Annie MP was surely her due or more than her due. These people were different, they *deserved* subjects. Their fathers were doctors and things like that. But she put her head in one book and lifted it only to put it in another, she left herself vulnerable between pages of immobile unknown facts. She narrowed down the space inside her head so that it could fit in between the other thirty-five strange pupils. She didn't want to be noticed or to get too frightened. She let the space get bigger when she read – opened it up just enough to learn what she needed to know, not too much in case she would forget it all. She believed at moments that she deserved subjects just as much as them. Sometimes she looked at other girls who looked poor too and hoped for them as well but mostly she kept her eyes down, sad and overcome with the huge responsibility for herself that had been put on her shoulders.

Her mother walked a tightrope that year as well. It was her job to move her child to what was possible, to steer her yearnings into the area appropriate to people of their poverty. A factory job, a shop job in a good shop, at most an office job or nurse, but she gambled and gave Rose nudges beyond their rightful station. Phyllis had always read since the days that her father had put all the magic letters in the alphabet together, made words and told her that there were stories, real tales, lives other than her own. And later when he was dead somewhere in those unconscious bitter flashes Phyllis had become convinced that there were books better than those in their mobile library. She herself mightn't be able to understand them all but if Rose was taught right there was no reason to believe she couldn't. Yet she had to be careful. Rose was her only child – and getting more likeable every day if she thought about it – and she didn't want her to shrink with disappointment. It was a risk to nurture expectations that might never be, perhaps the child would hate her. There were not many scholarships from this county and most of them went to townies. But nudge her she did, sometimes certain that this was the right thing to do, sometimes ashamed that she might be using Rose, sacrificing her to find out for herself what was in the books that weren't in the mobile library. She lit candles and prayed during the exam, she asked God to forgive her. The day the results came Rose was scalding the creamery can. 'Don't jap yourself with that water.'

The postman handed Phyllis a brown typed envelope. Rose stopped work and bit through her lip. Time stopped a century, maybe more, while they waited for the postman to go so they could have their hearts broken – perhaps not, perhaps not – in private. Once the first word was read – congratulations – they let out two screams, a shrill childish burst of joy that came from the throat, an older low moan of relief that came from below the womb and both screams came into one that stayed there in the air, forever, in that spot, as a monument to their pain and hope and dark poverty.

A year best forgotten about because despite its ending it had brought them nothing except a realisation of just how far down at the bottom they were and how worried they needed to be for a long time about what might not have happened if Rose had not got the scholarship.

It had been such a bad year that Rose had barely noticed she was in town, that she knew where two streets and the post office were, that she could find the bus stop without asking. Now she could notice all this and more. Secondary school did not fail her – they had subjects. The teachers did change at the end of each class – all these had not just been tantalising rumours. But the most amazing thing of all was that the pupils weren't hit. Not at all. It took Rose six months to believe this – she felt that sometime one of them would crack and would wallop her over the head but it never happened. It takes people a while getting used to not being battered – first they breathe easier, then giggle a lot, then grow tall and satisfied. As Rose straightened up and stopped flinching she learned firmly and forever that she did deserve subjects and not being hit. She noticed that the boarders did more subjects than the day girls, that they learned to play games, that they had special masses, that they mattered, yet she didn't let it worry her. She was getting her share of the knowledge and those petty graspings were only the concern of the anxious rich and their dependent church.

The boarders were the uptight daughters of Ireland's new rich men, and of women who believed completely in their husband's jobs. She was the daughter of Phyllis, of her grandmother, and of every dead great grandaunt who had wanted to learn to read. Starving ghosts of women stood friendlily behind her, peering into her Latin books, frowning with her when she couldn't understand something, nudging each other gleefully when they saw their county mentioned in history books, never once wondering why they weren't there with their brothers. Rose learned about Parnell (Charles, not Anna, not Fanny) Wordsworth (William, not also Dorothy) Connolly (James, not also Nora). She was not told about Mary Wollstonecraft at all, which was maybe just as well as there might have been trouble sooner rather than later.

Around this time Phyllis began to yearn unreasonably, not simply to wish, for the electricity. She wanted it more than she wanted water in a tap. She secretly wanted a washing machine. (Eventually all this happened – when the Fam washing machine arrived they stood before it slouched with awe, and Phyllis decided to churn milk in it before she used it for its proper function. The milk turned out lovely, the butter was near perfect but Phyllis couldn't wait any longer to see what the washing looked like. The hand wringer wrung the clothes perfectly, thank God they didn't have an electric one because your hand could get caught in it – women's, children's hands had. Once she did a washing in it she couldn't churn in it any more which was a pity.)

Rose had few problems living this double life required now of her. Farm work evenings with Phyllis and her father, refined school days when boarders talked of far away places, magic names, Moville, Galway, Monkstown outside Dublin, Skibbereen. Bet they had never once worn wellies. She had been well prepared by the Programme for quick switches from fact to fantasy. The wishing for what she couldn't have had been settled long ago, the time she had fallen in love.

Soon after Rose went to secondary school Phyllis had to see Sister Immaculata about books and uniform matters – stockings must always be bought from one drapers' in Dublin at eleven and sixpence a pair, the child must always have two pairs of shoes, one indoor, one outdoor, indoor ones to be left in school so they couldn't be worn out at home. Sister Immaculata looked at the awestruck lanky woman in the check coat and knew that she would do as she was told either because she would be afraid not to or because she would want her daughter to be as good as everyone else. After being dismissed Phyllis closed the door behind her, a pain in her chest, trying to remember some dreadful story about the priests that her mother had worked for. She stood in the cardinal red corridor and squinted with the dark, not knowing which way to go, but she pulled up her black puckered shiny gloves and headed left, determined to get out to fresh air where education people couldn't harm her.

Sister Immaculata checked her list to tick off which of the day girls' mothers she'd just been talking to.

Phyllis waited outside the gate for Rose, hoping that she wasn't too noticeable. She picked Rose out from the melee of distant girls by the way she put her coat on – she raised it above her head and let a sleeve slip on to an arm, then wriggled the other one down. Phyllis worried for her – all those well-to-do people – but she let go because she knew she could do nothing about the way things were. Phyllis was nervous about standing at the gate, maybe Rose would prefer to meet her on the bus, maybe she would be ashamed of her. But when Rose saw Phyllis she acted to her the way she did to not having things – satisfied. Her eyes lit up but she did think that she would make one improvement. If she had the money she would buy her mother a bra to wear the way all the town women seemed to. She was old enough now to notice things like that without being caught looking. And indeed Rose did buy the bra with her next birthday money – a flimsy teenage lace thing that wouldn't go near the right places on Phyllis but at least it put Phyllis in mind of it and she then bought herself a proper bra, giving the flimsy one to Rose who didn't have much need for it. In less than fifteen years' time Rose would try to get Phyllis not to wear a bra. They walked to the bus stop, Phyllis aware of the different kinds of spaces that there are in a town.

When they got home Phyllis said to Rose's father, 'Well, that's done.'

She never went near the school again.

Rose began to like town. The bus was half full when she got on it in the morning and there wasn't room to stand by the time it reached the end of the eleven miles. Part of getting sophisticated was finding out who all those people were who got on at, say, McElvaney's Lane or at the bad bend. Then you had to find out where they worked or went to school, if their parents or husband were dead. No husbands travelled on the bus, they had cars of their own or got lifts with other husbands. You never had to wonder whether a woman was married or not, they wore rings, but you might have to find out if someone was going with someone. Who was related to who? Rose could never get interested in these stories, partly because she couldn't remember who anyone was unless she had talked to them and also because she liked to decide for her own reasons not for pity, not for drummed up interest, whether she found someone interesting or not. She worried about everyone, but mostly about how women without rings had the nerve to live alone and she tried to imagine their lives – presumably they would have more time than others, more time to be lonely and more time to do what they wanted to do. On the bus she sat beside Clare McGuigan for the first half of the secondary year until the day of the row. Bríd Clerkin had been away on her honeymoon. Rose had always thought she was lovely – she liked the way her A-line skirt fell into points at the side of her legs. She liked her open eyes. She liked when Bríd took off her coat jacket. Her breasts were perfect. They sloped gently from under her arms and down from her neck into pinnacle shapes. How could anyone not like her? The day Bríd got on the bus again after the honeymoon Clare said: 'Doesn't she look lovely?' as people always say about a woman for a week or so after she gets married. They say it out of goodwill or out of an acceptance that she mightn't always, because presumably she won't look after herself now that she has achieved what she needs.

'I've always said that, not just today, but you never noticed before. You always just let on you didn't hear me. I hate the way people talk about people when they get married, as if they weren't the same as they were yesterday. I'd never get married to have people saying things like that.'

Clare squinted surprise – but mostly rage that someone might have heard Rose giving out to her. Why! She had no need to put up with this. From Rose, who was after all only from Doapey, or somewhere near there. Clare, who was nearly a year older than Rose and who came from near a town, had mastered sarcasm at this stage. 'No need to get your knickers in a knot, Rose, you won't have to worry, no one would have you.'

Rose was mortified both at the mention of knickers on the bus and at the obvious slur on her looks. She was also a bit shocked at her own unnecessary comments, what was the point in falling out with Clare over something that stupid? Yet it was started now and there was nothing else she could do but get up out of the seat and walk away – she was used to walking away in the fields and the fairly empty house at home, but where could she walk to on a bus that was nearly full by now? Blushing red hot she had to sit down again.

'A lot of good that did you,' Clare hissed, the winning mortification on her side. Rose had no answer. But she never sat beside Clare again. She couldn't very well. If she hadn't got up to walk away maybe they could have forgotten it, but as it was there was nothing much else she could do. She sat at the front of the bus the next morning hoping that Clare would say something but she didn't, not then or for a month, so Rose started going to the back of the bus past Clare's seat because she didn't want people to think that she hadn't the nerve.

The back of the bus was where the growing up happened in spurts. It was hard on the girls because they didn't always think the jokes funny and they had to sit around not doing anything. The boys could do things, they could bump into girls, even grab at them the odd time in preaccepted lunges, but the girls had to be outraged (even if they felt pleased or indifferent). The girls could touch boys with instruments – rulers, schoolbags, even bits of clothes like muffs or gloves, the sort of things that made individuals out of gauche teenagers, things as small as pencils, but never body on. The years were eked out of them, usually with much bluster and terrible embarrassment on the part of the boys and a lot of giggling from the girls. Sometimes when a boy would overstep the mark there would be a shocked unfamiliar silence from the girls – it was the dark shutter of women beyond which no one can go – but the girls themselves were still ignorant of what that silence meant. Yet by it they kept things under control, sometimes chafing at their moral duties but mostly accepting that it couldn't be left up to the boys. When the noise at the back of the bus got too loud, coming up to holidays or in spring-time, adults, and the teenagers who were going to be nuns or priests or goodie-goodies, stared down at the rowdy girls and boys and eventually quietened the fun by collective disapproval. But mostly a lot of giggling and unpleasant feelings and squeaks that had started out being statements but had failed, because of the breaking voice behind them, were put up with, all for the sake of developing heterosexuality.

'Wouldn't you think they'd have more sense by now?'

'Ach, they wouldn't be normal if they weren't at it.'

They had ideas of normality even though they did not know what normality was because they had certainly never heard or thought of an alternative.

Rose fitted into the back of the bus in the way that some girls were allowed to, as observers. She wasn't shunned but was rarely lunged at which was proof of something that none of them knew yet – how distance can be established by silence and hues of looks. She had left the panic notions behind her and fell in love selectively now, never bothered much whether love was attainable or not and certainly never expecting it to be. She was happy enough to watch others and to learn the codes of growing up by deciding whether their behaviour was contemptible or fascinating. There was never anything in between. To one part of an outside world that hadn't come near her or that she hadn't taken steps towards but of which she had heard whispers, she would be described as a young bird, a girl who wanted to wear mini-skirts, a future possible decorator of some man's side, table, bed. She felt that she should be satisfied that she might be any of these things, particularly a bird, but instead she felt uneasy.

Yet she dare not say a word about that – so she took it on herself and managed to smile at as many of the boys' jokes as she could understand and got off at her road, full of more new and wonderful things to think about, a twelve-nearly thirteen-year-old, getting pudgy in places, who loved her hard-earned uniform, unlike the townies, who were sophisticated enough even by then to relentlessly complain about the greyness, the awful blouses, the dreadful seamed stockings, and the length, the length of the tunic. The townies, at the end of each school day, lined up at the gates where they could be seen by neither nun nor boy from the brothers. There they tightened their belts painfully around the by now obsessive waists and worked the tunic up above the belt in deft tandem tucks thus shortening their collective uniforms by one hundred and eighty inches. In winter they did the same with their gaberdines unless they were leaving them slung casually freezingly open. Rose walked past them, not oblivious but not concerned enough to show two more inches of her legs, one hand always in her pocket, the squeaking of her case of books always in step with some quiet massive joy that was inside her.

Her two lives worked well but rarely impinged on each other. Fair days in town could have shook her up but didn't, because the wide scattered streets were too unlike the Ballybay fair to cause any real cultural tearings. On Ballybay fair day country-yard smells invaded the town and farmers cursed loudly, sometimes enjoying cursing in town, sometimes holding back if they wished a passing townie to consider them equal, sometimes enjoying behaving outrageously and so being what narrow townies expected them to be. Some farmers could turn narrowminded themselves in their own feelings of inadequacy – that was their only defence against what they believed to be their betters – better because of clean houses, running water, clothes, and the fact that they bought all their food. The farmers would have left early in the morning beating or gently tapping their animals into trailers or along the roads, trying never to think of their beasts, or the women or children at home grief-stricken about the gaddy calf, the friesian they had loved the look of. By the time town was reached any still weak-hearted man could work the emotion out of himself by looking at townies. Townies could pretend as much as they liked but fair days were there to remind them where the butchers' meat came from, to take them down a peg or two from their sanitised living. On these days the townies mostly tried to avoid the top end of town except for the adventurous ones and they were loved by the excited nervous buyers and sellers. Luckily for Rose school town fair day was different from Ballybay because she would have been a bit lost wondering which side she should stand with in these awful useless battles. Yet perhaps she could have worked it out because she was a pragmatic child – she had, for instance, decided to like de Valera. It seemed a small price to pay in order to have some one thing in common with her partially deaf father. She didn't know whether he – de Valera – was any worse, any better or the same as the other man and she certainly never questioned – because it wasn't considered important – what or even if he had ever thought about women. Liking de Valera was a means of drawing her life and their two lives together – she would give them back something.

Rose got her periods first in the class, at least she thought she did but she couldn't be absolutely sure because some girls didn't speak of these things in order that they would grow up to be the women who would not speak of these matters. It surprised her that she got them first because she was never first with anything – electricity, water, breasts or a tarred road. Some of the periods thing was dislikable – cuts on her inside legs where the STs dug into her skin, what to do with used STs in school, suddenly remembering during class that she couldn't remember where she had left the one she had just taken off, but mostly Rose enjoyed her aunt. (Phyllis also called it visitor sometimes, or friend.) It was another line to getting big. She didn't mind anything that was a line to getting big. She would never be big soon enough. Every day was just another day passed until she would get big. Really big. She wasn't quite sure when this would happen, fourteen, fifteen, twenty, thirty, fifty? She never went beyond fifty. But some months, the bad months her visitor rankled her, it seemed a heavy price to pay for getting big, yet on those months Phyllis would send her to bed with a hot water bottle and aspirin and look at her with some kind of ritual. Once, a bad month coincided with the picking of potatoes and she was let off gathering for the two days. She didn't know how Phyllis organised this with her father, hopefully she didn't tell him.

It was the first time that she had seen this other side of work that propped up those hectic days when neighbours flocked down on each other's streets to drop or to gather potatoes, to tie hay seed or to thresh corn. From the moment the men left for the field until Phyllis blew the whistle, Rose and Phyllis never stopped peeling potatoes, crafting the wild cabbage into a plate vegetable, setting places, frying bacon. (On the Friday they did fish for the catholics but still bacon for the protestants because they didn't want the protestants to feel that fish was being forced on them. Perhaps some of them would have loved smoked cod?) Rose had always thought that Phyllis just got the dinner ready for them all. As the men trooped back at one o'clock, Rose filled the basins on the doorstep and placed the Lifebuoy red soap beside them so they could wash their hands before they came in. They straightened and rubbed their backs after they passed on the towel to the next one.

The house was in a sense a better place to be, away from them, observing – it was also less hard on the back – but still she had cramps and was thinking about the woman she had seen jumping out of a car in Ballybay one day. The woman was cross, she dragged a child with her, not once looking at her husband, banged her door and bludgeoned her way across the street. The husband looked a mild enough man and unperturbed. She was cross and she had a car! So that was it. She had become a wicked little woman, too disappointed with the monthly round up of her life to venture a smile. Well then, why wasn't the world organised around periods – why not? No periods, no babies, no world. Sensible thought. 'Rose, wet the tea and lift them other plates. Don't put the yellow knives in the hot water – it'll only take the colour out of them.'

Another time, Rose, another time.

Chapter Six

The adult area that spread out from where Rose lived, sneaking up hills and hiding in illusory secret leesides, was a normal enough place. There was incest, battery, child molesting, prostitution (both recognised and not), sexually active priests, some women not married having babies and away, but these were only minor transgressions that came into the minds and lives of single individuals occasionally. If everyone had done them or even thought of them all at the one moment there could have been a serious upheaval. Tight reins were kept on all by an unawkward intricate web of lies, hypocrisy, a little goodwill, and the turning in unison of backs on troubled people. Perhaps the women felt sorry clenching their eyes tight on their own – because everyone was these women's own – but if they did they couldn't show it because of, well, because of himself. There were a lot of hills in the area, small intimate hills with clumps of pubic rushes running up them. There were whin bushes, prickly yellow against a sky that was supposed to preside over four seasons but that let them down mostly, and poured itself relentlessly on them. There were skeletons in cupboards, breathtaking lies and well kept up fronts. Few people cracked. They would never have lived it down so they held together outside no matter what.

All movement was monitored and the phone listener provided the vital missing pieces. The women made any important phonecalls that had to be made, 'Take it in the box missus', and while what they might be saying on the phone was not important it could drop some hints about things that were. The priests had cameras for eyes, mean minds, and little problem in knowing everything because people blurted out their most intimate thoughts, failings and loves (most importantly loves) in a cruel management process called confession. Rose no more than anyone else didn't have to grow up if she didn't want to because she could say she was sorry, would never do it again and it was as if she never had and yet she would know all the while that she would do it again and again, tonight, tomorrow. No one made traumatic decisions – they just went to confession.

There were drunks in the place and teetotallers. Men mentioned emotion to each other when their mother or a child died, women talked a little more, rattled conversations on cue that had not always anything to do with their real plight but sufficed to make them believe that they had friends. Indeed a woman was often convinced that she had talked about the real fear that was in her like a swallowing pit, when she had only been talking about the weather or the youngest's cold or the neighbour's youngest's tonsils. People pretended to their childlren that they were not unhappy, although they never actually faked sounds of happiness – there wasn't time. The women filled up emptinesses with masses and daydreams, rituals, and the teaching of manners and they slapped any child that asked an awkward question. Yet they clung to their children because with all their prayer and masses they had not worked out where and how they might go.

Some of the husbands could have been tender but they didn't have the words to get them over the first few years, the first few shocking rows, so they lapsed into hard men. Take Benny L. When he first got married twenty years ago to a woman with strange ideas he had jokingly called her 'Herself' when visiting a week after the wedding. She seemed half pleased, because she had to be, but wholly hurt. Because it hurt her and he did love her he didn't call her 'Herself' for years. But he had learned however what hurt her most. Now he never called her anything else but 'Herself' because whether he hurt her or not didn't matter. He had almost forgotten her name. For Cissy L's part, the jibes, the hating of all his relations, all his experiences, all his life, had only got to do with the desperate fight for herself. It wasn't really him she hated. His family wanted to drown her in him, in them, in little else. If she cared too much for him she could not care for herself. So Benny L drank and muttered to the floor in the empty bar. What could you do if you didn't drink? She had something to do – a war to fight, children to rear. He could only sit around waiting for his territory to be broken into. So he drank, to fill in the time before defeat. He didn't mean to deliberately self-destruct but he didn't try not to. If he lived to be an old unhealthy age then he would say that if he'd known he was going to live so long he would have taken care of himself. In the meantime while he was waiting to see how long he'd live he would drink and smoke on his own or with the others. And say things about 'Herself' that were then repeated by tipsy men to their sober wives who waited up to make tea when the men came home. Everyone knew what Benny thought of Cissy L. The women would have liked to spit on him but they remembered him when he was young and it would not have done Cissy L any good, and anyway no one had the nerve. Even the men who thought he went too far wouldn't have approved of spitting on him because if you let that sort of thing start you'd never know where it would end.

Rose asked once who was Mrs L married to. Phyllis said, 'Himself' and laughed at how quick she'd thought of that. Rose asked why she was laughing and Phyllis sighed, 'No why child, no why'. There was no point in talking about the too much sympathy women had for each other – it did no good, was useless in fact, and Rose would learn soon enough.

Then there was Cissy L's neighbour Mrs S who drank, publicly, once in a while. She knew now, after all her children, that there was no advantage in having a person running around looking like her. It had been too hard work that made her think of death, and she had lost for herself all possibility for everything or anything. There were bits of her – her eyes, her nose, the way she moved her hands when talking – walking around on different people. She had so many children there must be a complete her if the bits could be taken from them all and put together. She knew that there were not always two sides to every story and even if there were she only had to live one of them so that was all she could see, naturally. Her husband was out of the house a lot. She got so unused to talking about what she felt that she didn't trust words. Day after day in minutes, in her own silence. No wonder when she did take the odd drink that she made what they call an ass of herself. She poured everything out all over everybody in a waterfall of words that baptised them all – some for the better, most reluctantly. She had got married like the rest because it was what they did. The sanction on people's need not to be utterly lonely. The move into an institution, recognised by all others and guarded fearfully by all others. They called it a sacrament. By the time she discovered that she wasn't happy to be married she had been married for three years. She half said it – she was a brazen woman – and the others looked at her, knowingly, but furious that she'd mentioned it. She thought, so that's the conspiracy that has been going on. They nodded. But Cissy L patted her on the arm and despite herself said, 'You get used to it. There's nothing else out there anyway,' or some words like that.

And then there was Mrs W and her husband. They didn't communicate much about what they felt – which was perhaps just as well. Communication when it would come would be the ruination of many a marriage. They needed a stage on which to act out their stunned conversations – a few silent people to play to. Because there was no one, they said nothing and words began to dry up. But Mrs W daydreamed all the time that some night she and her husband would pretend that they were not married. And then they might like each other a little more. Rose knew that Missus was an important word, she had never been allowed to call a Mrs by her first name. But knowing was one thing and liking was another. She was often frightened by some hidden thing, probably the pretence.

But things were different in some houses. Packey and Minnie McArdle lived at the bottom of a wet hill. They were poor, getting poorer. Once they had owned thirty acres, ten of which were rushes. They got rid of that and bought sixteen acres, five of which were rushes. That was better because they knew then how poor they were. Before, they had always thought of themselves as owning thirty. Minnie preferred to know reality but Packey liked dreaming. Although even if she did like to know reality it wasn't a great thing to be acquainted with – the meagreness of what could be cheated out of sixteen acres and the work, the endless work to put nearly nothing on the table. They were odd anyway because she was older than him. Young women married older men because women the same age wouldn't have anything to do with them since they'd outgrown them a decade before. The men needed someone to be more experienced than, someone to be wise to. Also it would work out better at the other end of things forty or so years from now – she could look after him. But Minnie was older than Packey. People thought this wrong, their limp imaginations said autumn before spring, and the wrongness of it all made people out of Minnie and Packey. Minnie's sister had gone to America years ago to live an exciting life but as is usual things had not turned out as they should. Minnie's sister was only beginning to read that women could have orgasms and there was Minnie who had never left the townland having them and more startling knowing she was and what they were, although she didn't know the name of them. Not for her light shudders that could pass unnoticed during preoccupation about daily matters. She didn't have strange unfulfilled twinges that might merely raise a question mark – what was that? Just as well that men didn't talk or Minnie might have been in trouble though she felt sure that Packey could defend her. He had survived all the brutalising and was left with some emotion. He wasn't afraid. This one light battering against the grey was not because Packey was younger than Minnie but because Minnie was older than Packey.

Then there were the people who stayed single – someone as young as Rose would not have known when someone was definitely single, too old to ever get married now. Some of the single people had got so involved in other's lives – their mother's, their father's, their sister's, land, the weather, that when they decided to do something about their single state they no longer looked like the people they thought they were. Flushed faces, too fat, too funny about everything. Some men would not marry because their time was taken up in one long niggling competition with their fathers. Others married for that very reason and played out the same nasty games against different partners, hence the number of bewildered women.

But then there was a woman like Lily C who simply could not see why it was not better to be alone. She was smart, crinkly-eyed, well-dressed. She read books and had a car. She felt a certain kind of sympathy for the married ones but it often dried up because she could sense their pity for her, and what was the point of having sympathy for people so sick, so bent on forcing their lives, their bottomless mistakes, down her throat. Smart single women were often the daydreams of the married ones, they were independent, your own time, and possibility. But who would be expected to believe them if they admitted that? The same single women were the sharp slap to married men. Lily C in particular was hard to take because of the car.

Martin M on the other side of the chapel was much the same age as Lily but he passed mostly unnoticed. He stepped gingerly on the outskirts of family worlds – he could only send himself on threshing days while they sent sons (or daughters, if that's all they had) to him. He left them to think and say what they liked because how could he win if he took them on? He was somehow admired in a way that Lily C was not. His singleness was seen as choice, hers as failure.

Among the single ones there were undoubtedly those whose bodies and minds lusted comfortably and unacceptably for bodies and minds such as their own. They were muted, silenced, gagged or else they left with any others who couldn't stand the parish commandments. All single people were nodded to, talked briefly to and sometimes treated with neighbourliness, but always they were some signal that little things might not be right with the normal married state. And it was their singleness that worried more than their childlessness. Even Rose could sense that, because the married ones who had no children were definitely a notch up on the single ones. An unserious notch. Rose overheard when Mrs O'Brien had a child, 'Good on him. Now, would you look at Dermot Lillis, honest to God would you look at him. Not a child in the house.'

The men were to be congratulated or thought little of in the matter of babies being born, yet in many years from now when infertility was considered a problem worthy of real or feigned concern, it was women whose capability would be questioned first and sometimes first and last. But the problem that single people suggested was never met head on because there were advantages in having them. They acted as the litmus paper for success. In a place where men were expected by men to be distant, silent on anything that mattered, and part cruel, single people were the only thing they had against which to judge something of themselves or their success because some of the single people were so acceptable, the married thought that they themselves were even better. The fools.

Alongside this collection of the ridiculously self-confident married, there were widows. Some of them must have lived in their own houses but the only ones that Rose was aware of were the ones who lived in the Widas' Row. This was a grey heavy stone line of houses paid for out of some obscure protestant purse – anything protestant was obscure. To Rose, these widows were extraordinarily lucky – they had been married, now they weren't, they had their houses and they were unusually happy-looking, neat trim women with perms who bought their own newspapers. Behind their collective front there were the individuals who had broken down at gravesides, their hands across their hearts, their knees giving way under them, water that was too abundant to be called tears flowing steadily from their eyes, thus satisfying the attendance at the funeral – providing the talking point for the gawkers, assuring husbands that they were well needed and hinting at wives that they could be worse off. There were also those who had looked out, tearless, into the distance at the trees, the sky, whins, anywhere but the gaping grave below them that was going to be home everlasting to the only person they'd ever loved, even if in

65

some cases that was a long time ago. These tearless ones left an unease over the village for a day or two, an unease that was in fact well disguised alarm. Putting all the widows in the one row of houses took care of a few essentials, the one commendable one being the looking after grown people who had never had a penny in their lives that could be called their own. The more suspect reason being the grouping and discardment of a number of individuals whose only point in common was that they had been the women of men. Rose didn't see that the widows were now filed away bodiless, given a mock reverence that had nothing to do with them and their loneliness but everything to do with respect for the dead men, the husbands. She did notice that widowers were different. Firstly, they lived in their own homes. There were two of them – respected men, sympathised with, who could put no foot wrong because a man in that predicament could be expected to do anything – drink too much, neglect children, or whatever else. Noel P had shut himself into the house for six months after the funeral and drank whiskey. The neighbours looked after the children. Now, if it had been deceased Mrs P, who is to say or not say, what would have been thought. Or said. It was a wonder with such low expectations and with such instant forgetting of the dead mothers that the children of widowers turned out as any way well as they did.

Then there were the rumours. The girls, the young women, around whom hung immovable rumours, slurs that stuck like rats' dak cast against them *once*, thus becoming a fact that rattled in the air every time the woman's name was spoken. It could have started with her going to England for a year to work but not looking appreciably better off when she came home. It could have started with a postmark that was in blatant disagreement with where they said she was. Or she may have fainted in the chapel a month or six weeks before she went away to work. Or her mother might have been away for a few days without saying where she was going. Or they just knew to look at her – the women anyway. A plumping of her bottom, a drooping of her breasts. An aged, unconsolable look on her face.

'She'll never be the same again.' And indeed if the rumours were true she wouldn't. Her child kidnapped from her for life and given to what was accepted as respectable and at the end of it she wasn't even credited with character or courage. There were many, many, many more than a dozen women whose lives had been destroyed forever by man and by rumour. And then there were the facts, the facts, the women who could not be rumours – the women who without husband had and kept their children. They were few and far between because although they could not be stoned or burned anymore they could be mentally twisted on the spit each day, hammered on the anvil, booted in the cunt. That word, the word indeed whose mental picture was reserved for violence. The dirtiest, most insulting, most powerfully outrageous secret that there was. These women reared their children in a wondrous cocoon – a safe bird's nest woven together, made warm with an unimaginable love. A sort of blind innocent love that was edged with daily courage. 'I do not care what they think. I do not care. Even when my child has to go to school, never. Even when I go to mass, never. Even when I go to the shop. Never. Even when the child gets sick and they say . . . Never. Not this morning. Never.' It was a cruel wicked battle of nerves, her against them. Them with right on their sides, they thought, her soiled with the only sin that mattered. Obviously there were men tiptoeing around passages to hell – it was accepted, yes, it was, that a woman could not get pregnant on her own – but they were easily forgiven – one confession, then all right, all right my son. It is surprising, suprising that more men were not killed in the middle of the night.

There were also three postscripts. Three married women who lived alone – two of their husbands working in England, celibate no doubt, the third one whose husband was remarried and living as near as County Down. This last family put at the foot of family death notices – there had been six in the fifteen years since he'd left – 'Rhodesian papers please copy'. The poor man, they said, had to go that far to get work and it's much too far to come home on holidays from. Down they dug their necks in the sand that was really muck.

It was among these inadequate stances that Rose was growing up, but luckily she didn't know yet. She was free to believe still that she lived in a place where things just happened, because people made them happen, a place where all action and all dreams were not predetermined by harsh rules, unwavering poverty and pagan fear. But she was beginning to have flashes. She put them down to her periods. That's what they were – that's what everything else was – her visitor. 'It's only your visitor', and every other girl's visitor. That's what caused all the trouble. Women and their visitors. If they hadn't those flashes before their visitor came, everything would be all right. And then there were those other moments – when she had her visitor – she would be lying in bed with a warm jar on her stomach after taking two aspirin and she would get more than a flash, it would be a clear vicious picture of meanness, only the falling sensation caused by the aspirin and the hot jar would stop her from screaming: 'Now I know, now I know you bastards.' 'It's your visitor Rose, your visitor, all women feel like that.' And so the women around here got cross, because they saw, they knew a little more than their men.

On the bus one day Tessie Duffy's nose started to bleed. She sat white and near to tears, holding a soaking wet handkerchief to her nose. The girls rooted in their cases for Posies and more Posies keeping the supply up with the dripping blood. The boys stayed near silent for some time, then Louis Brady flexed his muscles and said with an arrogant sneer, 'If they're not bleeding from one place it's from another.' The boys roared laughing, slapping their legs, pushing their big ugly noses into what wasn't their business. You could tell which of the boys didn't know what they were laughing at because they joined in a few seconds late. Maybe some of them didn't want to be part of the crushing mob of boy-men. But if that was the case, it didn't show. They would never be able to know what fools they were unless in a decade's time some of these very girls broke it to them gently – not in so many words of course.

'If they're not bleeding from one place it's from another.'

Tessie Duffy gagged on blood and what her bleeding nose had brought down on her and all the rest of the girls. If her nose hadn't bled they would not now be bunched here exposed. The girls tried to continue the conversations they were having or they looked out the window apparently so engrossed they'd heard nothing. Two of them who had been standing up when the words had been said rushed to their seats as if blinded. If they were sitting looking ahead at least they would not have to look at the boys. A collective blush spread up their necks, burning their humiliation into the atmosphere. If only a few of them felt a need for revenge, all of them, every single one of them wiped Louis Brady out of their lives, their considerations, forever and that was as powerful a thing as they could have done. You could feel the ripple of erasure as it worked its way down the bus, down his throat and spread outward from there melting him away. No one would marry him now.

Chapter Seven

Rose was used to aunts and uncles and cousins coming on holidays. For six weeks in the summer they came in dribs and drabs, interrupting the work, causing moments of brightness and an occasional row. These were people who had left, had to go because there were not enough bar jobs, building jobs, office jobs. (Some wild ones went even though they had jobs, because they missed an older sister, brother or friend.) They were the brothers, the sisters of Rose's father and Phyllis – anonymous numbers who got lifts to Cork and went from there to New York, Boston, Chicago or the bus to Dublin and from there to London, Liverpool. Going away had its advantages for some – men who wouldn't have been touched with a forty-foot pole at home managed to get married away because they were Irish.

There was one woman, Mamie – sister of Phyllis – who went to Belfast, which in the end was to become further away, harder to understand, than New York. Phyllis and her were close though, because they both had one daughter.

Rose's favourite was the one she had seen only once – the one in New Zealand. She had two children and came on holidays with them, her husband didn't come. Who is to say that she had a husband at all? No one ever saw him. But they did believe her because surely no one, no one could have that sort of nerve, and if they had it was best not conjured with. Phyllis was easily flustered when she was there. Phyllis said that the children had no manners. The aunt said 'Phyllis, Phyllis we must give them their independence. They're individuals.' With talk like that she wouldn't have a soul around her in twenty years' time,

Phyllis prepared herself to sneer. But Rose had smelt her, watched her, and hung on every word. The aunt stretched and sighed. 'Life, lovely life. Rosie, dear, when you're my age you'll be able to do what you like. Things will have changed. Mark my words. I was born a small bit too soon. You have no idea, no idea what you'll all be up to when you're my age. Free. You'll be free. Hah, at least you'll think . . .'

Rose understood the spirit not the innuendo of what she was saying. The aunt quietly said to Phyllis the day she left, 'I won't be back. Them O'Gormans still blame me for putting the idea of New Zealand into their son's and cousin's heads.'

'They don't blame you, it's just that no one else had ever gone there before.'

In a way she had been to blame, although the circumstances left her little choice. A man who was to marry her changed his mind so she had to make it as far away as possible. (It was also a dramatic touch and much more enviable than New York where everyone had a cousin.) The man was married now, but when his people ever heard New Zealand on the news they thought of her and viewed his marriage with a whiff less seriously than it deserved. During her holiday she asked Phyllis several times, 'Which one is she? Where is she?'

Rose said, 'Where's who?'

Phyllis went red and poked her.

'There was no need to do that, Phyllis. The child doesn't know what we're on about.' At mass the next Sunday Phyllis said grudgingly, 'There she is. The woman in the black pillbox.' Her aunt peered.

'Poor woman,' she sighed.

'How many are there running around?'

'Six.'

Her aunt giggled at the thought of it, obviously pleased that it wasn't her. Rose could only half figure what was going on but she enjoyed all of it.

Her other aunts and uncles, even grandaunts and granduncles, came too – Yankees, they were called. They came to convince themselves that home was remaining backward. They were horrified to hear that there was running water near the village, although they didn't let this show; they despised signs of mental or material progress because why then had they left. All the while they gave clicking noises of approval but you could see reticence in their eyes. They blessed themselves passing the chapel to satisfy others that they had not forgotten; at home in New York they talked of quaint religious customs. They went to mass as if to a personal investiture where they could see and more importantly be seen by the parish. They walked straight-backed, white teethed, the women dressed indescribably, the men in ghastly plaids and wearing aftershave. The patchwork of people that despite itself worked its way through the year, became frayed at the edges in the light of their scrutiny. Individuals felt ashamed of their clothes, their hair, their false teeth, their children – who could have been better looking. It was an unequal scrutiny because the Yankees knew where the Brianses, for instance, lived.

'Still in the old house? That little house, my God. How do they all fit in it? Is the thatch still on it?'

'No, they got rid of the thatch years ago, ten, fifteen – yes fifteen years ago.'

'Ah, what a pity. There will soon be no thatch left.' The Brianses did not know where they lived – was it a large house with a sitting room as well as a parlour, with a view of the sea? New York's a small island, isn't it? Did they eat in a room off the kitchen? Did they have a telephone or two cars? Or was it a dark noisy flat beside a railway station, looking into another dark flat? The Yankees never had to say if any of their daughters were pregnant on their wedding days – the people at home blurted days and dates out. One thing they had to admit (they couldn't very well not because it might catch up with them and the others would then mutter, 'How well they didn't tell us *that* while they were bumming').

'Margaret's Kathleen is dating an Italian. I suppose it could be worse. At least that's one problem you don't have here.' And they silently sent their hearts out to Margaret – the little bits of them that were left after thinking. 'That'll put the blowing off her'.

Rose wished and wished and wished that they had that problem here. Italians, blacks, Jews. She would prefer all of them to anyone pale. They would know things, other things. She was certain. She did wonder about the half-caste problem – they had mentioned it at home before. 'That must be the worst thing out. That must be terrible, altogether. Neither the one thing nor the other.'

She could just see them, one half of their bodies black, one half white.

'Are all children born half-caste if one half of the parents is white and the other black?'

'Oh yes Rose, all of them.' What a pity. And what a pity that mixed marriage here was such a colourless affair.

When Rose was younger than fourteen she had worked harder at her jobs when the Yankees were around. She felt proud of the work, the amount of it – the number of different jobs to be done, the hardship conditions. She was blind – fooled hopelessly by Yankees fawning over reward, over the health of it all, over rosy cheeks, into believing that these jobs were indeed romantic. But this summer she didn't like them watching her – maybe seeing up her skirt when she was bending over, smelling her clothes that whiffed of cow's milk and other things, looking sympathetic when some job made her frown with effort. Why if it was so great had they left it? Why if it was so great could Rose, her father and Phyllis not go on holidays to New York and be attended by these people? Of course the attendance would not be so difficult for them. There would be running water, they would not have to carry an extra bucket, boil kettles, to bring basins of lukewarm water, soap, 'not in the basin, it'll be all mushy' and towels to the bedroom. Rose was learning about something for which she had no name. She puzzled over the feelings of resentment she now had towards the Yankees and when she could reach no satisfactory conclusion as to why, this year, she felt overwhelming spasms of hatred towards them, she sent her mind off to find a word to explain how she felt, or rather why she felt what she felt. But the dictionary had thousands and thousands of words and she had no idea where to start. She didn't know the word and without the word she was at a loss to know what she felt.

Mamie and her daughter came at the beginning of August. This year it had been arranged that Rose would go down to Belfast, which was north of here, with them on their return, for two weeks. At last. This promised holiday to the city had been a long time coming. Mamie and Phyllis tucked in to chat, aches and pains, their daughters, mutual acquaintances, past times, their mother (a fact that Rose always resented. To talk of Granny like that!). Rose was left with her cousin, a pale-faced, modern, beautiful child who was two years younger than Rose but who knew everything. Absolutely everything. Being from the city. Actually she was a spoiled, pasty-faced child who did her best to be nice most of the time, even though she'd never been taught how, but who knew how to camouflage ignorance by fair means or foul. She was not going to let her self-confidence be shaken by this country cousin. She stepped around the far end of the meadow where they were making hay, she didn't have to work so she didn't. Sometimes she wandered over when Rose and her father were twisting ropes, she'd ask if she could do it, and he would let her – the job that Rose liked best. But in the strange way of country people Rose forgave her because although she believed that she knew everything she also felt sorry for her when she watched her awkwardness out here in the fields. Rose could slip the iron rope twister through her hand all the while thinking about other things, she could step back the exact distance in precise movements, leaving the hay that was now rope at the correct tension, all the time daydreaming, unaware where she was. But Yvonne got the hay tangled, hurt her hands, slacked or tightened too much, got fussed and then more fussed when she began to rage because her gawky, country cousin could do something that she couldn't. She would then stomp off, Rose and her father would glance at each other in some secret communication, that was as mysterious to themselves as to anyone else, and the work would go on.

74

The work went on as if it had a life of its own – the people, implements and the horses were only pawns in the raising up of cut dried hay into haycocks. Once the people (Rose and her father in the morning and Phyllis in the afternoon) came into the field they set about work involuntarily, enslaved to what in the end was only fodder. They turned the hay, facing its wet underside to the sun, in neat rhythmic motions – the movements of women. They shook out any of it that was in laps, swinging wisps of hay into the air as if they were raising an imaginary monstrance at benediction. That task done, they contemplated the field, figuring where to start, unaware that they were now prisoners of the smell that they had thrown up. They could not now leave the field even if they tried. They would be drawn back hypnotised into the communion that was going on between the sun and the dark underside of the hayrows. That done, the man would then sit on the shiny seat of the rake, the horse would pull wildly, pleased to move, shaking her head of flies. For a few moments Rose could hear nothing but the heavy click of the handle as raked hay was dropped cleanly in rows. She could dream then, until the whole field became a field of neat lines. Then they would gather, shake, throw, handrake, stamp, and top. The rope was created from a gentle feed of hay that Rose's father guided on to the twister, watching not to feed thistle in, one end was knotted firmly to the haycock, the rope was thrown over the cock, jiggled as in dance movements and finally secured. The tension of the rope was checked. The area round the cock was raked again, tidied as clean as a kitchen floor, and then they could look at their work before heading off to the next one. (One up one left to go, one gone one left to go, – haymaker women were good in labour – they'd trudged through those lines before). Farmers had choices at this moment. Where to put the next cock. They would often turn together, out of sight of each other at the other end of hills, viewing feet, yards, lengths of hay, before saying with a certain satisfaction, 'This spot'll do.'

Four, maybe five, cocks later Phyllis would come with the sandwiches.

Phyllis, Phyllis' husband, and Rose would sit down under a scant bush. It might be bad luck to sit under the thick hollowed out hedges because that shelter was only for the teeming rain. Phyllis would put the sandwiches down on the drying cloth and pour tea from the tin sweet-can. (Sometimes she brought the tea in tall white emulsion bottles.) They would eat the sandwiches – skinned tomatoes, lettuce, scallions, egg, salad cream, mixed together to make a tangy taste, as if surprise, wonder and satisfaction were the sisters of hunger. Phyllis and Rose's father would talk, loudly at first, then their voices would slide into lower tones, murmurs. Strangely, her partially deaf father could hear these secrets. Rose would lift her book that was always brought stealthily in case her father was cross with either Phyllis or Rose and so not inclined towards chat.

'Does she ever take her head out of them books. Soon she'll not be able to talk at all.'

They would rub or touch gently their sunburn. Normally there were only the three of them – but this week there was also Yvonne. She was bored – (Rose didn't have the nerve to be bored) and had been bitten by a cleg, a red bite sat as if mounted on the white base of the sting. Yvonne hated the vulgarity of haymaking. She was too enlightened to have this backwardness pushed on her, she knew about The Beatles, she knew who they were going out with and she knew what 'You Don't Have To Say You Love Me Just Be Close At Hand' meant. Phyllis and Rose and her father knew what Yvonne was thinking. Her whole personality would have flaked off her body, crumpling in little bits before them if she had realised how well these country people could read her. Rose smiled at her, forgetting the fuss over the cleg bite – if *she* got a bite she didn't tell because there was no point. Anyway, that gushing sympathy for her cousin was sickening. Yvonne smiled back – she could be nice sometimes when she forgot how important she was.

It was a pity that the Belfast ones had come to them first because by the time Rose set off for their house Yvonne and she were sick of each other. Yvonne had seen one full week of Rose, yet again, in that most unflattering of places. She had updated her impressions of last year and yes, Rose still thought that the Top Ten was as important as (once she had thought it was the same as) Top of the Pops. She still thought showbands were the same as groups, she clung in her ignorance to country sounds or individual voices. She knew no words of songs Yvonne could sing and whistle. Rose – a girl – wasn't allowed to whistle because it made the Blessed Virgin cry.

Rose did in fact know one song, 'These Boots Are Made For Walking And That's Just What They'll Do, One Of These Days These Boots Are Gonna Walk All Over You.' She had sung it along with the wireless one Monday evening at a quarter to seven. Her father had been startled and had switched off that noise. It must have been the tone of her voice that had annoyed him. It was indeed the hint of vengeance that made her like the song. Vengeance for what, Rose? They took photos before they left and of course, of course they had to take one of the horse. Phyllis took the pictures, lined the glass with the sun and pointed the box at them. Yvonne hated having her picture taken. Rose was mesmerised by such confidence. She would have liked to pretend that she also hated it, but at the last minute a need for immortality would come over her and she would smile or at least look serious in a serious way. Phyllis took the one of the horse with a reverence – she knew that someday horses were going to be a sign of wealth, though how she could have figured that out was anyone's guess, considering that they were now the hallmark of the tractorless poor. By the time they reached Belfast Yvonne had managed to create a kind of contempt in the air, but the next morning she relented and spent one full day with Rose, introducing her to friends, shops, names, roller skates, double-decker buses. After that she drifted away to particular pals that she had obviously decided to keep to herself. All these unharmful avoidances were possible because of the spaciousness of cities. For Rose it was like the first day out after being ill. She was left to her own devices with no work to do. All she had to do was come in for her meals and go to the shops, which wasn't work. For two whole weeks she wandered.

Sometimes she stared at her aunt Mamie working the hoover,

a machine that sucked in dust which couldn't be seen in the first place. Rose stood around the doors until Mamie made her sit. Mamie was uneasy in the presence of this quiet, distant child whose cheeks were surely too rosy to deserve a sad look like that. She shushed her out to play, Rose didn't understand that she could go out to play without being told. Also she liked watching Mamie. If only Phyllis had a hoover – a carpet. The street was full of people, people not even saying hello to each other because they would have too many hellos to say. It was wonderful. Rose sometimes made even more people because she counted them, first in one whole persons, then in bits. She found herself once counting one, two, three, four, five. One two arms, one two legs, and a middle. It multiplied even the large number that there was, made the noise louder, started loud musical sounds in her head. She was dizzy on bodies. There was a continuous bus screech from her aunt's house up to the Arcadia – a windy shop that smelled of fresh white bread, Brussels sprouts (a small cabbage-like vegetable) and brandy balls (a round brown hard sweet with white stripes). There were other shops, in other streets, some with open fronts, and tiled floors. Every single day women went to buy vegetables, potatoes, something for the dinner. Even if they hadn't wanted to go daily, they would have had to because they fed everyone on found money. Each night or morning they juggled or foraged and found sixpences, half-crowns, which they brought grudgingly to the shop for foods that Rose thought should have been in their gardens. But who was she to talk, her father moaned to the high heavens over potato drills reluctantly conceded to carrots, parsnips, cabbage, beans, curleys, peas and one year beetroot – that put the tin hat on it, who needs beetroot? 'How many do you want kept this year?'

'Four or five.'

Phyllis would get three.

At the shop they talked of bigotry, their husbands' work, their husbands not working and signs of trouble to come. They whispered some things, hands over their mouths, voice directed out of the corner of their lips. Could they have been scared?

Belfast had up to now been two things for Rose, smuggled butter and a man who stayed in Duffy's sometimes. Smuggled butter sat in yellow pounds inside the door on random mornings – it arrived from nowhere unexpectedly. So did the man in Duffy's. He was from Belfast some time ago, that much Rose knew, but the rest was vague because Phyllis said that's what happened in Belfast.

These past pictures of Belfast intruded on Rose only when she saw the women whispering at the shops, but mostly she forgot all aggravating intrusions and saw only new tender exciting things.

Frances lived one, two, three, four days away from Aunt Mamie's. She noticed the stranger but couldn't be bothered until the fourth morning, when company would do her no harm. 'Hey wee girl, are you from the country? Do you want to come to the clinic with me? I have to get its orange juice.'

Rose went without saying a word. What could she say to this frightening colossus? She walked silently beside her, swallowing a lot. Frances was taller than Rose, had thick hair that was parted on the left side, drawn down to her right ear and wrapped around it. A selected, apparently casual piece of hair would then drop down over a half ear. She said little the first day, too preoccupied, Rose presumed, with the task of pushing the pram. The clinic was another tiled building, Frances stripped the baby expertly and put it alongside other babies in a straw basket where it screamed unmercifully. A nurse said, 'Fourteen pounds, four ounces.'

Frances dressed the baby, the nurse handed her a bottle of orange juice. Rose watched these movements – women dipping up and down, dressing, undressing, sticking dummy teats into mouths, talking, talking, mesmerised that they could have established such a stunning ritual around the rearing of babies. A streak of buried begrudgery in her thought it was no wonder city people were stuck up and spoiled. They left the clinic, Rose chastened further by the importances that these people could claim, not knowing that they were getting mere drops in a 'Vitamins Will Fight Scurvy' campaign.

'Where are you from?'

'Doapey', although she wasn't quite.

'Where's that?'

'County Monaghan.'

'Where's that?'

Frances shrugged her shoulders. So did Rose. Rose would have loved to do that with her hair but she'd had such a row about a fringe – Phyllis had finished in the that's-the-end-of-that voice, 'It's cheap.' She wasn't going to do anything dramatic like this or backcombing.

'You can come up the mountain with us tomorrow.'

Rose felt a flush of gratefulness, she promised herself she would never forget this. Now she would have to ask her aunt, which she did, but failed to say, because of the self-preservatory wile of people who want their way, that Frances was coming too. She didn't know why she hadn't mentioned Frances but her ignorance was indeed well founded and her cunning without malice.

'Yeh, go ahead.'

Oh lovely. She went to bed with happiness, excitement and fearful edginess. She told Yvonne, half hoping that she had achieved some social success but Yvonne only shrugged.

'Them ones.'

Next morning she called at Frances' door – she wasn't asked in. She could hear the mother and father barking sentences at each other. There was a wicked tin edge to the mother's insults, the only possible sharpness left to a woman who had thrown her life after someone she knew damn rightly she should never have liked so much, young or not. Frances and she walked further up the road, no child in a Tansad today, to call on more closed doors, collecting a bunch of nameless boys and girls, all in or around Rose's age. Frances talked today, gabbled about all sorts of things, what they had done last week, what Joe Carr had said once. She was a good describer, threw her hands about a lot and said funny personal things like: 'Poor wee me.' She had the confidence to draw the world around her and see that it was opposed to her.

'Poor wee me.'

She also had one false tooth which helped to make her more mature. She read 'sixty-four-pages' all the time. These were thin romances that lasted around sixty-four pages. As well as all that she wore a pointy bra. Rose wasn't allowed to, Phyllis said that her father was giving out about the last one but Rose suspected that it was Phyllis who begrudged her that little bit of grownupness. Her father surely would not have the nerve to say anything about a bra, even to Phyllis.

An extraordinary thing happened up the mountain that day. Rose got a crush on a boy who was imperfect – he had too many freckles. (How could anyone have a crush on a boy who was imperfect? Was this Rose realising that all boys were a little imperfect or was this Rose growing up to believe that she would have to ignore some minor or major inadequacies? She didn't know.) He also had watery eyes that made him look childish and sexy in turn. The curtains had not been drawn when he had German measles. But Rose got a crush on him. His name was Matt. They walked a long way up the mountain, winding in and around heather, looking down on waves of red roofs. The sun shimmered between them and the city below. They got tired and some of them sat or lay down. At this point Matt made an obvious point of staying near Rose – sensing some possibility. Rose was too young to know if this was a mean selfish lust or an honest desire for the two of them. In fact she was too inexperienced to know that there was a difference. As they walked down he worked his way closer and closer to her until the inevitable happened. Inevitable, because Rose was coming to an age when she felt ready to be kissed – not to kiss, of course. She realised, in fact, that she was a little late, some of the girls in her class were already going on dates with their coats open, some of them could sport love bites on a Monday morning, but Rose simply couldn't allow herself to be kissed if she didn't feel like it. She knew that she would have the experience sooner or later, there was no rush, she wanted it to be special, not any old kiss. A tall perverted nun had spoken to them in menacing tones of a friend's devastation, and rejection of course, on opening an expensive present – a bottle of perfume – to discover that it had been used. Only the bravest dared titter. What if it was only sniffed, not used, Rose wondered unconcernedly. She knew the nun was referring to things more serious than kisses – still, Rose would like her first kiss to be special. She could only think of kisses, the other harsher ends of male-female mating didn't bear thinking about. Her first kiss should be beautiful – indeed Rose, that's not too much to ask.

It was beautiful. He was the same height as her so there was no craning back of her neck, consequently there was less chance of bullying, even if he'd wanted to and it was doubtful that he did. Rose stood there, he rubbed his face and lips around her face and lips in a most tender unexpected way and soon Rose got used to it so she put her arms around his waist and kissed him back. They stopped kissing and both hugged each other tight, half imprisoned by their delicate smells, unable to move. They were warm. If he had done one thing wrong then, which was what boys usually did, shoved his tongue into her mouth or bitten her ear, it would have destroyed it all. As it was he was either innocent enough or brave enough to leave china shop mistakes for the football yard. They came from behind the rock, wordless, no one would know that they had been kissing, it had all taken just a few minutes.

A few minutes to change her from the unkissed to the kissed. She was right to have expected so much from a kiss. She smiled a secret smile without parting her lips and could have cried for joy. What should she do now? Would Rose tell anyone? Should or could she describe it? She would have liked to tell Yvonne but that surely wouldn't be advisable. Frances? Perhaps not, perhaps she had been kissed years ago and would dismiss Rose's kiss as babyish. (In fact Frances was a mother. That was her baby, not her mother's, but Rose didn't know this. At least not consciously.) She would tell Christine, Matt's sister. That's what she would do. That would be beautiful, just right, a stab at playing families. But before she could say anything Christine told her that another boy, who had been up the mountain with them, Maurice, a hateful boy, fancied her.

'Me?' said Rose. 'He couldn't, I don't like him.'

She was struck speechless by the cruelty of growing games. Obviously these people went around fancying people all the time, never with any particular reason. The thought that he, this horrible mean boy, could want to be able to kiss her put the whole idea of crushes and kissing in serious jeopardy. She let Matt slip quietly out of the throbbing part of her eyes, chest and lower lip. Funny, he himself, or he the dream, put up no fight over his dismissal, maybe he felt wicked over their closeness, maybe he, the dream, didn't stand a chance against the sudden grabbing back of her body. The night that Christine upset her she rubbed parts of herself that she hadn't touched before – under her arms, her neck, her skin. Lightly. She had of course had furtive dark enjoyment years before this – all of which had been completely erased from her memory with the advent of purity and Blessed Virgin-ness and Maria Goretti and her teaching. How could she, an ordinary girl, have the nerve to stand up for the truth?

She left Belfast wanting two things – to be a protestant (she had decided that they were freer, although why they had to make people so nervous she couldn't figure out) and not to be from where she was from. When she was home for a few weeks she decided against the protestant bit but she set about tidying up her own place. The row with Phyllis was brewing for two weeks – the citified Rose was cranky and impatient, Phyllis knew that there was an unacceptable change. Rose simply could not tolerate all the bits and pieces. She was not going to put up with it any more.

Sunday dinner Rose said, 'Altar rails are going out everywhere else.'

'How could altar rails be going out? Don't be stupid. Where would we go to communion?'

'I'm not stupid. And we never even got to the stage of having communion linen.'

Phyllis glared nervously. This really was too much. What Rose had meant to say was that she wished they came from a city or a town at least. She wished they didn't have to get wet all the time in winter, or spring or autumn. She wanted to be allowed to go places for half hours, or hours even, without having to say where she was. Phyllis jumped from the table, pushed Rose, accidentally or not, and roared, 'Close your mouth.'

Well, that was the end of that.

It had been a while since Rose had vowed to hate Phyllis for the rest of her life and after. And after. She went to her room and wouldn't cry. But in time daily living couldn't accommodate such hatred, so although the memory was still there they got on with fiddly life, eating, school, working, sleeping and some happiness.

Chapter Eight

That particular summer Rose had gathered clandestine words around herself and learned them with a sense of wonder. Words usually take with them ideas, ideas can be more of a problem than words. She could stop using new words if Phyllis disapproved too much, forget she ever learned them, non-exist them by lack of use. But ideas were less easily put down. Still, a person could always have ideas, even troublesome ones, without anyone knowing they had them. Particularly a person like Rose who was used to self-conversation. The ideas were seeping down into her, darkening her sense of outrage at the order of things, propping up her sense of poverty, and making her believe, without any possible reason, that she and hers were as important as the next – as important as townies or city people – although never of course as really important. She had decided years and years ago – three years to be exact – that she was suffering from nostalgia. She'd read about it and certainly she felt those exact longings, not of course for things past, rather for things possible. She'd also read that Scorpios were obsessed with death which was why she was terrified every time they cleaned out the back hall.

When they had cleaned out the back hall, scrubbed the floor, washed the windows and took them oul' dirty milky smelly coats from the pegs in order to give the door a rub, they exposed the Civil Defence book that was hung by a string under all the coats. She told herself that her terror came flooding over her because of her stars and not because of the war that was going to happen any day now. If she told herself that often enough today she would be able to sleep tonight. The stars had possibility. She was in the throes of trying to explain herself to herself and why not stars? Religion was handy too when you believed in it. But increasingly she had moments of niggling doubt – nothing serious of course – it was no laughing matter, loss of faith. The cardboard green prayerbook, the butterfly thin gold-rimmed missal, the benediction, incense, the getting of souls out of purgatory, hell, who could dare? How was she going to understand herself, save herself?

She sometimes lapsed from these important questions into the panacea of the newly-discovered 'sixty-four-pages', called that because it usually took sixty-four pages to lead the woman to the altar. This is as she meant to do, it was one way of stopping those dreadful unnecessary questions. 'What do you need to know for?'

She would fantasise about drowning and being saved by a tall blond man. It was difficult, because the sea was not part of her life (and no swimming pools had been built around here). She'd seen it – the sea – first on a tour to Giles Quay – a cold grey astounding spectacle that went into the sky on one end and moved relentlessly, hopelessly towards her at the other, never getting there. But then she'd get tired of these peculiar stories, no one could believe that a man could make you that happy, unless you were happy to begin with. The priests were talking about God knows what and the people didn't understand them. They were never meant to. Limbo was still there but the percentage of dying unbaptised babies was dropping so there was something to be thankful for as always. Some years later they did get rid of Limbo – this black bottomless hole – but they never told the mother's of the holy innocents, they kept it to themselves as specialist information to be bandied about at large oak tables and in sterile sacristies. Rose's compatriots around here were by now walking happily down roads, letting their feet eat up distance, waiting for bushes to kiss under. Her day-girl town school friends were similarly searching, only for them it was alleyways and doorways. And Rose was letting it all slip past her, noticing only that terrible things were beginning to happen, or rather that terrible things happened always and that now no one could hide it from her. Like one day she thought Johnny – remember Johnny, Rose? – had been treated like a dog by all of these people, every last one of them. A dog – a man's best friend – patted on the head, given food, left outside the door, 'Put that dog out will you.'

She wore her blouse back to front under her cardigan to pretend she had a polo neck. Anyone could pretend anything to everyone except themselves. She wanted to be holy, holier, holier in a different way, but what was holy? Everything that was holy was perverted. Everyone holy was wrong, wrong. Nosy cold people. Half of them were beating their children at home – not hitting them, beating them. It was the place of the terrified. Few children loved their parents. Love? Love? How could they. Their fathers would have died rather than hold a child's hand – if you held their hands you could not hit them and hitting them proved love better than holding hands. It was hard indeed to work out what holy was. Impossible. Christmas morning the priest would extol children to love their parents because perhaps the fathers had got out of hand the night before. He had to do something to smooth down the fast heartbeats, the headache, of upset women and children and he could hardly upbraid the fathers. They were next to him, both above and below him. They were too near for censure. And that very nearness ensured that there were few askable questions. A person could ask the wrong question and get hit. Rose was treading a very dangerous path. And difficult, because she did not want Phyllis or her father to know, they must never know. She was after all lucky – her mother's desire for education was not a mean one. It was related to knowledge and dignity, not to gombeenism. And her father let Phyllis know best. Look at the Reillys. They too were going to secondary school – (now possible even for the scholarshipless poor, poorer and poorest) – but they got into serious trouble at home for talking about school and their mother had to try to stop them in front of their father. He had stopped talking to them in anticipation of what he believed was going to happen – his being left behind. He was

right. They probably would have stopped if they had understood what she was getting at when she butted in on their
stories. If she'd said, 'Look, you father doesn't think you should
be going to school. I do. So to make it easier for me with him
would you mind not blathering on about it as if it was the
United Nations you were going to.'

But she didn't say that, she said wash the cans, clean out the
byre, and get water, whenever they looked set for a conversation about school events, the events that daily were building
barbed wire barriers between them and their parents. So they
blathered on. Rose was lucky. Or luckier.

A singer blared 'You're much too young girl' in an attempt to
hold back the generation that wanted to know everything now,
and wanted to stop or start everything now. 'Later later later'
he pleaded. Rose thought about later. When's later? Never you
mean. Later Phyllis said. Never you mean Rose thought and
gritted her teeth, thinking I'm as far away from you as the stars.
That satisfied her because it seemed such a dismissive thing to
think. She rushed around the house in the evenings wanting to
change things – the angle of the floormat, the place where the
egg basket was kept, but Phyllis moved slowly after her and
changed them back again. Phyllis now had the semblance of a
home, the sort of place anyone could run to with a new baby,
any woman looking for order and history. She was not going to
let Rose undo her silent creation.

'There's a lot of goat's hair in them clouds.'

That night the wind made hearing inside the house nearly
impossible.

'There's a new moon next week.'

The chimney whistled and they moved closer to the range,
warm and cosy and so lucky not to be outside. Relief and heat
bound them together but the binding was fragile for Rose.

'That's a desperate storm. It wouldn't be a good night to be
out at sea.'

What would they know about the sea? Her father had never
even been to Giles Quay. Her mother had been to Blackrock
only twice, both times on sunny days. Why did they have to

keep talking about weather and things they knew nothing about? She couldn't remember one new conversation here. She conjured then what it would be like at sea, she tried to know what she knew nothing about, these wanderings in her dreadful arrogance she denied her parents. But her mind – before she had a chance to question her own unreasonableness – returned because here inland there was enough to worry about without adding unknown problems.

'There'll be a full moon after that, I think. Give me down the almanac till I check.' Full moons. New moons. Tides. Comings and goings regular, regular. Her visitor was regular too. Perhaps they were linked? Perhaps the moons and tides and blood flows were all linked. The moons continually disturbing the seas rushing them this way, that way, the tides in their anger sucking blood from every woman. Ah! now she had something to think about. She smiled again. It was easy when she had something to think about.

Poor Rose. She was a little lost. Phyllis and her father had solved their questions long ago – there was never any doubt but that God made the corn grow and hooshed out the sun in time to save the hay. There was no need to go further than here, despite the damp. If it came to the bit what were rushes except thin aubergines, not that they knew what aubergines were. But the damp was terrible for Rose, the wet, the muck, the depending on good summers to get the wellington marks off her legs. Now of course if she was allowed to wear trousers this would not be a problem. Her smile disappeared again into the hard raging line of her thin lips. Her friends were not hearing questions either. Their hearing was taken up listening to advertisements for deodorants and anything that could spray, spray, spray. Hair lacquer. Plastic things. Not plastic sandals, they were for children only. Plastic other things – coloured plastic raincoats to flash before their eyes on wet days. Why have raincoats the colour of rain? Umbrellas with new springs, coloured umbrellas. Rose wore her scarf loosely tied. On cold days she brought the ends round to the back of her neck and knotted them there making a pumpkin out of her face. She could never remember to take the umbrella.

The school went on retreat. It was wonderful that no one could talk to her. This must be what it was like to be dead. She was peaceful about the worst worrying of things. She made resolutions, not to do with vaginal purity – which was what the whole retreat was about – but about her questions. She would keep them coming. Every answer deserved another question. But if there were only half as many answers as questions she might have a better chance. Still she was not going to slip into alcohol or religion induced deep sleep, just to shut out reality. She thought that on a brave day.

Rose began to concentrate on seasons, weathers, as a way to calm herself. Why not? A white freezing morning she walked to the bus, her hands aching with heat inside her gloves. The film of ice cracked under her feet. The silence was so acute, like disappearing thunder, that people could be heard shouting morning orders as far away as half a mile. She could hear the wild swans before she saw them screaming out staccato the mournful pleas of Lir's children. She watched them flying on and on, with tears swimming in their eyes no doubt, against the icy wind in the triangular formation that they'd made for themselves. They swapped places gracefully, the one who had to take up the front letting out a loud gasp, the relieved one letting her echo blend sympathetically. Rose knew that the lake they were heading for was as frozen over as the one they had left but she couldn't break it free for them because it was miles and miles away. Yesterday a pigeon came and sat mournful and tired, on the same branch all day too cold to move. The robins had picked the crumbs with the minimum of gratefulness – the starving have little time for pleasantries. Rose decided that it wasn't winter but rather the beginning of a scorching hot day. She did this because she always wanted what she hadn't got and because in dark winter it was harder to escape. Conversations became closed to fit the rooms that everyone was forced to crowd into for warmth, cooped up, getting on each other's nerves. In summer there was more light, less words with more meaning, a better possibility for concentration, so she made it a summer day. There were flies and other flying insects, the cows were in a bizz, going wild down the hill instead of standing dirty and stiff in the byre, throwing their legs and bodies out from themselves to stop the warble fly driving them mad. The sun was making people bold enough to long for unreasonable things – holidays, happiness, love. The doors in the house were all open, there was no washing hanging in front of the fire. Phyllis was wearing a yellow striped frock with a slight patch of lace at the collar. You could see the hair under her arms. They were spraying potatoes, smelling bluestone, Rose peering into the bubbles felt half buried in the copper barrel mesmerised as she was by the extraordinary uncopyable green. Her father walked the drills with a back sprayer showering potato leaves and specking himself so he looked like a man with blue measles. Or better still it was a spring morning and everyone, everybody was in good form smelling flowers and sighing with relief knowing that they had a long stretch now before it could be so bad again. The lambs were there defying her *not* to write about them in her essays. Why, only yesterday she had put her hand into a dark warm bird's nest, her fingers had tingled as far down as her knees. Or it was autumn, warning all just *how* bad it could get and Rose was picking leaves and pressing them between the pages of her books. They were faithful and complete, as like herself as any of the people she knew. The birds were nattering on the electric wires discussing routes, nodding gravely at the people they had to leave behind. Funny how, like the people, they'd got used to the electric wires – where they had converged to leavetake before the rural electrification scheme? But autumn brought her back around to this morning. It was bitter cold but at least it wasn't raining. Rose often joined in with the saving sentiments of this place, 'at least it's not' and 'thank God for that anyway.'

Although it was Monday she didn't have to buy a weekly anymore. The man had given free bus fares with free education, because he said that there was no point in giving free education if they couldn't pay to get to the schools. He knew what he was

91

doing, removing the last possible excuse that the parents might have. The free bus fares removed a dangerous power that had played itself without cue at least once a week between Phyllis and Rose. Rose would not want to do something, go out in the cold for slack, run down there and check them cattle, get an extra bucket of water just in case – just in case what – that a busload of holidaymakers arrives without warning. Rose would sigh and who would necessarily blame her, who that is under the age of sixteen. Most times Phyllis let the sighs pass but sometimes she said 'six and ninepence for your bus ticket. I'd take for two pins and leave you without it.' Rose wished her mother would stop using that nonsensical 'I'd take for two pins' and she'd try to concentrate on that rather than on the serious possibility of not having a bus fare. Phyllis had never not given Rose the bus fare. But the threat would work its way down through her dignity layers and she would cry about the unfairness of such power, power to withold bus fares. As Phyllis saw her crying, – whimpering it was, whimpering – she would lose her head balance altogether because God knows it *was* hard to get the six and ninepence and because Rose, by crying, was denying her the right that she surely deserved (control by threat) and anyway she hadn't meant to say that again because it always seemed to upset Rose so much. She mustn't say it again.

Rose got on the bus. It seemed full because of all the extra jumpers and coats, mittens, caps, scarves. The air was stale – some would not have brushed their teeth on a freezing morning like that and many had withdrawn into sleeping postures and smells as soon as the bus heaters warmed them. She began to sit down beside Goretti Mohan and was immediately sorry because she remembered that Goretti's older brother was supposed to be dying in the County Hospital. He had swallowed some binder twine that had, by reason of having a life of its own, worked its way into his sandwich and it had either poisoned him or wrapped itself around his gut although they were sure that this latter was unlikely because he couldn't have swallowed that much without noticing and he would have a big gut now, being a grown man, not like a child. It could be called a farming accident. Rose was sorry that she was now half way sitting, her bottom and knees bent, because she wasn't good about death or near death, particularly in the mornings. What could she say to Goretti? Nothing. But she had to sit now that she was here so she did and they talked about lively enough things.

'I was sitting beside Goretti Mohan this morning.'

'And how is she? As well as can be expected I suppose.'

They made the most that they could out of people being sick.

'He's not the best really.'

'Ah now he's improved. You should have seen him yesterday, if you think he's bad now.' They made the most out of death too when it came, except those who were closely affected and they hated the spectacle. Rose didn't realise that older people had to do this with death. There was nothing else for it except to build nuances around the funerals, frivolities, and right things to do. Everyone was talking about Goretti Mohan's older brother.

'I doubt he'll get it tight.'

'I'm afraid you're right.'

Funny, it got his grandparents out visiting again. They dropped in on people on their way back from the hospital.

'That's something I suppose.'

That's what they meant when they said, 'It's an ill wind.'

Something else they said around here was that it would freeze a brass monkey. There were no balls in these houses where children were growing up. And it would freeze a brass monkey in the weeks that people were visiting Goretti Mohan's brother in the hospital. Rose's mother and father went too.

'We went the half too soon. He's not as bad as I thought he was. There wasn't a bit of call for it. Yet.'

They would have preferred to go when he was nearer dying, unconscious at the very least, because they wouldn't have had to look him straight in the eye or imagine that he knew they were there. They wouldn't have had to see him thinking, people in my life older than me who are going to live longer than me. If they'd gone later they would only have been doing the right thing by those left behind. They wanted to do that and it's as much as could be expected from them.

'He was prayed for at the chapel today.'

That settled that and indeed it did. He was dead the next morning. It wasn't that he died – he was dead.

For the young people funerals were wonderful – perhaps they would be touched by it – they were fascinated by the nearness of death. Adults, at least properly grown adults, were too familiar with it, they didn't want to court it. But this was such an untimely, tragic, indeed laughable, death that all the gawkers for parishes around came in their droves. They lined the chapel avenue six deep pretending not to be there as voyeurs, pretending that they were there in support and sympathy, but some of the people in the back rows couldn't stop themselves standing on tippy toes, not when the coffin came out as might have been normal, but when the mourners came out.

'She's not doing bad.'

'She might be all right now but wait till the grave. That'll be the death of her. The grave's a killer.'

Half a dozen of them rubbed their hands and waited. Perhaps they were mortally nervous but Rose wouldn't allow that.

'God he looks like death himself', but they didn't linger too long on the men, it was the women they had come to watch. How would they bear up? And when the first woman did cry, something like relief shot through them. These proud spectacles were human after all. They could be got at. A young lout put his arm around Goretti Mohan's shoulder and played protector. All she needed was air. She looked at some light clouds that were creeping over the hill blacking out whole parts of the earth and leaving hilltops suspended in mid air with no bottom to them. Floating static hilltops. She ignored the lout but he didn't know it. Rose smiled.

'It was a big funeral. The biggest ever. You couldn't count the cars.'

In life facts this was their way of being sympathetic, of weaving death into everyday things. They had to do it even if they hadn't wanted to because everyone knew about death here – there was no shunting off of age groups so every death had to be dealt with, separately. People had to believe more in God in these places. But Rose was sixteen and she wasn't going to let them away with an inch. She believed in their insincerity and perhaps she was right but if she was, she was wrong about one thing – they were no worse than any other townland or village of people.

The snow came soon after the funeral, the proverbial white blanket bringing warmth with it and a comfortable hush. Their footsteps followed them around and were most definitely not there until they made them. People enjoyed walking – the history-making of it, the plush sounds of their footsteps echoing in their ears, just as if they were walking on carpets. Dark-haired people looked well, the grey-haired looked steely against the blinding white, red-haired were warm, only the blonde looked ridiculous. The first day the pathetic ones threw snowballs, people so ignored by all and sundry that they would do anything to be noticed. Even if they were disapproved of it would be better than not being seen at all. The second day layers of accepted groups joined in, somewhat like war, and by the third day the notion of snowball throwing was accepted by all as inevitable – indeed fun. Society gone mad – you could bend over, pick up something – it could be as small or as big as you made it – and you could throw it indiscriminately or at a specific person. Weeks – maybe two weeks – when you could throw things. It was a relief for love-stricken boys, this was how they showed their love and what an easier way to do it than by having to talk. Many a girl was pelted wet and was expected to know by this how big was his notion of her. Some girls accepted this code language, not because they liked it but because they knew that it was all that their particular fancies could master yet. Others bristled with disdain and made the boys worse. But the good thing about snow and snowball-throwing was that the girls could join in, if they really wanted to or if they were really pushed.

Sometimes the fights were fun, sometimes they verged on a show of hatred. Boys versus boys (these were the serious funless ones). These were re-runs of boxing matches. This was war. Big boys battered little boys and little boys were told to grow up and not to cry. Occasionally girls fought girls, halfheartedly, it would turn out later that they did this by reason of being excluded from the major fights or because one girl felt sorry for another who was going home not specked once with white. Once in a blue-mooned white fortnight you would see a real war between the girls but it always came to a sharp end because no one knew what to do about this most extraordinary unexpected aberration. The main fights were between the rippling middle of boys and girls. And in these they played their roles pretty much as how they would live their lives or at least how they would like to live their futures. Anyone with half an eye could see who was going to be what – a girl who liked being beaten by the boys – she would think that a husband should always be more intelligent than his wife – a girl who didn't. A girl who sometimes wanted to beat the boys, a girl who always wanted to beat the boys – a girl who didn't. The girls who wanted *all* the girls to win, the girls who didn't. Few went for draws.

Rose had generally taken part in snowfights, straddling between always wanting to beat the boys and sometimes wishing for naïveté but this year she approached the snow with an inexplicable viciousness and freedom. She didn't even wear gloves. She went from one fight to another, a fight at the bus stop in the morning, fights all day every possible chance, six fights on the way from the school gates to the bus. She bunched snow into balls furiously, her hands going blue and she slung with a force that she certainly didn't recognise either as her own or as an inherited trait. She didn't care who hit her or how often or how hard, as long as she hit back, or hit first. People noticed her — they thought she had in some way gone mad, they particularly noticed her blue hands. She would have loved to throw the balls at windows. The thought of shattering glass held a certain promise. But she hadn't the nerve, so she stuck to people. And the thaw came in time. Bringing with it a vicious wet cold as the atmosphere sucked the snow into tiny particles.

Chapter Nine

Perhaps it was the death, perhaps it was her age, her growing pains – who knows? But Rose changed drastically following the funeral. There were no such things as phases or teen age in these parts in these times so it must have been the death. Not particularly Goretti Mohan's brother's death but any death. Sometimes death affects, sometimes it's just the closing down of a furnace, the shutting tight of a gate, tight so it can never be opened, nevertheless merely the shutting tight of a gate. A job well done. This time, this death broke loose fizzy things in Rose's head. She held her head, rubbed her forehead as if she had a headache but it wasn't a headache, it was explosions. She went to school the following day a little more alert than normal, as indeed was everyone else – the way people from relief or fear, perk up, waken up, liven up, sharpen up, when tragedies happen. When she reached her stop she decided not to go to school. A sudden illogical decision that did not come from a real desire not to go to school, more from a wish to mark with something other than complacent drudgery annoyances that she felt. It was the last day of part of her innocence. She walked up the town against the stream of dawdling blue blazers that moved down the town. What would she do now? She had no book with her, school books yes but not a book. There was no one else around and she had to watch in case some nosyparker would report her, not that they could be completely effective in this instance because they would not know her name. Would she be able to do it? Day-girls who came from the town sometimes mitched but that would be for a purpose. No one from the country just stayed out town. Would she manage it? She succeeded until lunch time. Half a day spent walking aimlessly around the town, looking at how they worked, talked, lived, noticing how quiet they were really. She went to her classes after lunch, aware that she had now started another world for herself. A quiet illegal place where she could welcome sensation as a valid part of life.

This had been coming anyway – the death had merely hastened it. And if she was going to mitch then she might as well smoke. An early morning cigarette in the public convenience would pass some time and make her head so light that she would welcome a walk. And smoking, even buying singles, would mean doing without legitimate things and so she would have to deceive because deception is the flip side of having no economic independent means. But this was to be, there was no other choice. She had long gone beyond some of her classes. There were other things to know – facts, fictions other than they were teaching her. There were art galleries mentioned briefly in *Stair na hEoraipe*, places where you could see nude paintings, so many of them that you'd get used to it. Of course if Rose was there she would act sophisticated, worldly, and hopefully no one would hear her swallowing. There were the Salem Witch Trials – she'd seen somewhere that the bishop had said in Boston that he had in fact told a lie – what *were* the Salem Witch Trials? There was Kitty O'Shea, was Kitty really her name? All that wonderful nerve she must have had. There was the reason that the history nun could support the French Revolution even though they were against God. There was *something* about women – lots of things. She could never put her finger on it quite right. Something about women – what the nuns had felt tied inside those box faces when they were not allowed to show their hair – why were they not allowed, why did women have to cover their heads at mass, why would a bare-headed woman insult God, what *was* so wrong with women's hair. There was travel, the checking off of imaginations against reality. She hadn't even been to Dublin yet. Belfast yes. Belfast, and remember how that had been. Dublin would be even better.

Maybe. Now *there's* something she could have done with all those Yankees – she could have asked them what they meant when they said 'it's a different life over there.' She could have bled them instead of crawling away ashamed, because she had believed that different must be better. It was really they who had thought that different was better and she had not the nerve to disbelieve them.

Yes, there was more than she was being taught at school and she had a good mind to find it out. And there was also what was going on out town. She could think these things on the street. She would join the County Library and spend the useless classes there instead. Or maybe just on the street if that's what she wanted. She would live away from and outside of the shadow of sad Maria Goretti who did as was surely right and died for it. Sad saintly Maria Goretti haunted Rose. She hated the name Goretti. She had to put up with Maria, there was so many of them. What she lost in the classroom she would make up on the street. She had in ignorance started a self-education. Her intentions were not artificial, her desires had gone beyond her own knowledge. She had tapped in without knowing it to questions that were blowing up in other places also. Places far away from here. She had become part of something that had nothing to do with her. And Phyllis would be so sad if she knew. That sometimes stopped Rose but she was sure that she loved Phyllis enough so mostly it didn't stop her. Phyllis would not have understood if she'd known but she should have, because Rose's intuitions were for expansion and she hadn't lifted that off the ground.

Eventually – with all the mitching she was beginning to be noticed – a boy from the Brothers asked Rose to the café. She wasn't particularly fond of him, she didn't know his name, but she wanted to go there and she couldn't go alone. If she wasn't so poor and had a reason to go there, for instance to get chips at lunch time – instead of eating sandwiches at school – banana sandwiches, banana sandwiches now inferior to chips, then she could have easily sidled into it as the townies did, but to go there without excuse, no. But now she was there.

And this was another new life. It would be the saving of her because here there were illicit unfettered friendships. There was a juke box belting out sex and gyrating hips, at least that's what it appeared to do to Rose. It had a round glass smooth top – like half a world globe. A girl could want to lean over it and slide her arms across it, sighing and dreaming and aching for some damned unknown thing. For the first few weeks of her café times she felt half lucky – who would ever have thought that she would now be sitting with these townies, these people who knew nothing of dark roads, weighted silences, and outside toilets. It must be her face she thought, because it couldn't be the rest of her. She had developed a certain equalising attitude to parts of herself – her hair was greasy but then it shone beautifully after she washed it. (Phyllis would not let her wash it every day and what a waste those greasy haired days! She didn't go to the café if her hair was plastered to her head, naturally.) Her legs were short but then the calves of them were smooth. Her hands were too big but then her nails weren't flat. The only part of her that had no antidote was her bottom. It was colossal, spreading all places, working its way down to her thighs and making them bulge where they should have been tight thin, the appendix, of course. So she tried not to think about this end of herself and succeeded mostly. She thought about her face, which she'd heard described by an older girl at school as attractive. That was better than beautiful because it had some mystery to it. Beautiful could be sickening, pasty, but attractive was always two steps ahead. Yes it must be her face and it was a great place to be, drinking one tea and eating one snack spreading the affordable out over an hour, maybe hours, smiling at boys, laughing too loudly, believing that gauche, awkward gauche was the prize of grownupness.

But after some months of playing cool, putting her head to rest on her arms, pretending she was bored, yawning from too many cigarettes, even turning up late for the boy from the Brothers – that was the bravest thing because she could have been left alone in the café – Rose began to get edgy. She began to notice and in the noticing the magic left. There the girls were, in or out depending on a hair parting, playing a waiting game, some more happily than others. The waitress in her nylon mint striped coat looked like some other woman who wasn't and would never be a waitress but that could not be. Never. That was not allowed to be. Every pound was not as good as the next one. Waitresses did not look like women who weren't waitresses. The waitress looked vaguely like Phyllis also. But yet what could Rose do? What else was there? Particularly here, perhaps anywhere. So she went for a long walk with the boy, he knew where the trees were. They kissed under the warmth, it was too expected to be wrong. They came to an open field – Rose had not known that there were fields this near town. They unintentionally lay down beside each other, he leaned over to kiss her again and she pulled him over on top of her. Without knowing why. A flash, like inevitable lightning once thunder has struck, shuddered, then exploded through her heart and head. She screamed lowly and tears went down her throat. She blessed herself inside. She would have done anything, gone anywhere, she cried tearless with thanks but he was startled and gently said, 'Now come on, no.'

Perhaps he knew better, more than her, perhaps he knew less or was more sensible. Who knows? It was just Rose's good luck that he put his arms around her, sat her up and said no. Which was fine with her because she was too happy as it was. She looked past his shoulder and counted buttercups. She thought of all that needless space out there. All she wanted was a small piece around her because she could make it as big as she wanted, could paint stars in it, could explode it into silver. She held his hand and they walked back into town unembarrassed. She would always remember his name now. They dropped hands when they stepped out from under the last tree and she got on her bus, child turned woman for one moment.

After that she went walking with him often. She let herself be led by an 'It isn't often that I'm out so I will' attitude. And she began to believe that she deserved this too. Presumably now she'd be living on a short comeuppance but still it was worth it. And yet just as quickly as she loved she went off him. It was the colour of his socks. She couldn't, not with someone who wore white socks. She couldn't and she didn't but she never did forget his name.

Really what happened was that the effect of the death was wearing off her.

She had to leave the café then because she couldn't stay watching him. The meanness of the human who cannot stand to see its leftovers eaten and enjoyed. She didn't know she was mean, she simply, indeed simply, thought that she would choke with panic. The café had perhaps outrun its joys for her anyway, so she went back to classes.

She never did forget his name.

Rose's return to seriousness was helped by the taking of the census. Something as final as that can make a person take stock. The forms arrived, creating a sense of history. They would enjoy this. They would find out things about themselves. As was proper the Stair* teacher took her job seriously and used the opportunity to explain about previous Irish 'Censi'. The first one, the last one, the significance of, the political uses of, the guaranteed confidentiality – absolute guaranteed confidentiality – of. She stressed the last point so much that as is the way with people, they began to doubt the confidentiality of. She explained that in some areas in Ireland the Guards collected the forms, indeed filled them out. Perhaps this could be because the people could not write. Write or not, you could surely find someone other than a Guard. Hah! There would be no question of that around here. 'We'd better fill them things out before the Guards are on the door-step.'

People got dog licences here for the same reason. Never give the Guards an excuse to come out of their barracks and delay on your step. And so they all sat down house by house around the blank pages, prepared to fill out the most private of details, prepared to fill out the whole form although that wasn't necessary because so much of it didn't apply to them. There were sneaky questions that made the women snort and the men

* *Stair* is the Irish word for history

102

nervous: 'State the number of rooms occupied by the household (including kitchen but excluding kitchenette, scullery, bathroom, toilet, consulting room, office, or shop)'. Naturally you'd include the kitchen. Didn't you live in it? What bathroom? What toilet? Consulting room for the doctors, that was alright, I suppose. And the one about the motorcars. Motorcars, not even motor car. Oh dear. Why did they want to know when you finished school? It was a little too private. But they got to know things about themselves. It gave them a chance to tease because writing themselves down made it all more real. She was indeed married, they were indeed living here now, and their children would never know that they had lived elsewhere. They checked the forms over, and whereas before the married women wanted to get it done, wanted to see it complete, now they were vaguely irritated because there was so little of them mentioned. They felt a slight uselessness as they looked at the documents, something to do with not having their names on it and when they saw their children's names down here under his it seemed a little unfair. They felt something like Abraham's wife. The one whose son was to be sacrificed by his father to the father. No one ever asked her how she felt. Their work was not even allowed to be that, it was called a duty and it couldn't be included under the status column because you couldn't say that you were assisting, unpaid, a relative. They closed the forms. Phyllis thought, what else would you expect, and then made herself think how good her husband was. The men became cocky for the rest of the week while the forms lay there waiting to be collected – they had been reminded who was head of the household. Beside their cockiness the women were hurt, they had got a small slap, just a tap on the shoulder, the little sign of what it would be like to get a kick in the cunt which you could just get if you went too far, indeed if you went anywhere.

Rose looked over their shoulders in a vague sort of fashion at the completed forms. She saw Head of Household and imagined that even in Gilligan's house the father was there in that spot. Gilligan. Mister Gilligan, if you wouldn't mind, was the local child annoyer. Rose herself had been cornered three times, her heart had nearly stopped as this giant walked closer and closer to her, displaying hands from every part of his body. She couldn't even scream. All she did was close her eyes and forget. It was known about Mr Gilligan. Mothers and fathers steered their daughters away from messages that might cross his path. His comings and goings were the best charted of any person around here but still he managed to meet girls on roads. On a good year he could touch every eight-year-old within a five-mile radius and he had many a good year. There were few between thirty and thirteen who'd not had his warty hands on them, or in and around them. Head of Household. Ideas sometimes became facts for Rose and in one moment, watching the census form being closed, watching Phyllis put it between the tea canister and the delph dog, she imagined every man, whether related or not, being Head of her Household. Weren't they the ones who always ate the tins of salmon as women and children looked on? The thought was so horrifying that it would have to be one of those facts which are ignored, so she ignored it, which took nerve but still it was a thought that had become the truth.

When the forms were all collected and sent off to a Dublin office to be made into statistics things returned to normal. The days, weeks went in, by, and Rose was sometimes itchy and annoyed, sometimes calm and full of goodwill. Phyllis also. Phyllis' annoyances were of course more serious because after all this was Phyllis' life – real life, whereas Rose was only growing up. If Phyllis could have believed that she too was only growing up, if she'd known that in twenty years time she would look back and see that yes there were possibilities then. If. If. Only growing up – only. Only. That means there's better to come, it's not all finished. If. If. If only. Some days Rose and Phyllis' annoyances came together, the two of them bloated, expectant, waiting for their own tides to go out with the moon. On days like that they snapped at each other's heels, Rose knowing that Phyllis was determined not to let her live one single privacy and Phyllis knowing that Rose would eat her up and still want more of her. They would go to bed – Rose to solitude and hate, Phyllis perhaps to love, although Rose wouldn't have suspected. But to compensate, more than compensate, sometimes the calm fell down over them both during the same night. They would wake up in their different rooms curious about each other and that was the greatest thing they could give. At breakfast Phyllis would say and did you sleep well you should always make sure to put the hot water bottle in early in fact on nights like these you could take two bottles really. And what subjects have you got first to-day. Rose would answer, History and Latin, I love Latin are you going into town this week? And Phyllis would marvel at a young girl loving Latin, a priest maybe but her Rose! Rose would put on her blue shiny scarf and Phyllis would say you'll need another scarf soon, and in their farewells Rose would feel that Phyllis clinging was all right, in fact it was perfect, and Phyllis would believe that Rose would do her proud and protect her in her old age.

Phyllis would work well on days like that because to love Rose she first must love herself. One morning she thought again, yes Rose will always be here but a shiver caught the side of her body and scraped itself up and down her, reminding her that she had thought that about someone else once a long time ago. Oh my God she whimpered and an old lightness filled the top of her head. She touched her face and she could feel up as far as her eyebrows but there was nothing above her eyes, yet she could feel her hair. The emptiness moved down the back of her head, went into her shoulders slowly eating down her body until she was nothing except a face and two wild hurt eyes. She could see the trees outside, could hear bird noises, could smell her kitchen but she was nothing. These outside unimportances were assaults on her grief. He, the man she had trusted, had told her that he did not love her anymore. He couldn't quite remember when it was that this had struck him but it was more than a fortnight ago and he wasn't one himself much given to commitment or working at things because if you had to work at them it wasn't worth it so he wouldn't be seeing her again. He said a lot more but Phyllis didn't hear. She folded into her hurt. It was a long year. She remembered there were three different types of days and in each month there were thirty or so days. There was a crying day – she would go out to a field – there was not any talk of her walking death – she would gulp shock, loss, grief, letting some more salt tears out of the bottomless well that must have been there unknown inside her all the time because surely it could not have been created by someone else. Then there was a raging day – the going over what he'd said – the nerve of him! the sneakiness! the spinelessness! the skinny snideness, better off without him. Then there was a nothing day. A numb nothing day. And then a crying day. She walked the roads, the fields, a year of her life, while others looked on and hoped that she would soon stop living every second of her waking and sleeping, because there are too many seconds in a day for any human being to go through. And the unexpected minutes of reprieve did stretch into an hour, hours. She stole minutes not to wonder what he was thinking, not to pray that he would change his mind. When the year was up – 194- – she never let herself say the last number – she had killed the spot in her brain that corresponded to it – there was again only one day in each day and the types of days sometimes ran into each other which made time pass easier.

When Rose's father walked home with her she thought, I am walking home with another man then said a man not another man. He was kind. He asked her to marry him. He wasn't dangerous. She would stay with him until he died or she died. There was a war on and Rose's father, before Rose, offered something other than fear and gnawiness and also whatever it was that was love in the 1940s.

It was because of these things, her experience of cold secret loneliness, this hidden past death unremarked upon, that Phyllis could and did pass through life gently. Her daughter would be educated and that, that, that monstrous humiliation could never be so bad for her. A bird skimmed from the tree to a lower bush and looked at Phyllis, reminding her that there was a bigger world than hers spinning around on time and leaving the past to the past as best it could. She put two brown eggs in a saucepan, covered them with water, lit the gas ring and steadied the saucepan on the flame. She filled the kettle from the crock of spring water and pushed her hair back from her forehead with the resignation of one who knows that tears are a luxury. She went down to the bedroom and would have loved to put her arms around him and say something tender or better still for him to put his arms around her and when she would not respond him to say cajolingly Phyllis, but because none of this was possible she said your breakfast's ready and he said good girl yourself.

While they were eating breakfast the postman came, a fat man with a deep purple face and a lisp. He puffed off his bicycle and went to the door glaring at the sniffing dog. The dog rolled his sniff into a tentative snarl but when the postman glared back he changed his mind and sniffed again. He attempted a menacing uncovering of his teeth as Phyllis opened the door but a reprimand from her sent him scurrying defeated to the back of the house.

'Great day.'

'If only it keeps up!'

The postman walked in and Phyllis poured him a mug of tea.

'Charlie's not too good today. I was just up at it. The door was closed.'

'Is that so. Don't think he'll make it.'

Rose's father stood up. Some mornings he hated death. The waiting for it, the watching of other people getting close to it. He also wanted to see what was in the American letter, from his sister. The postman drank his tea slowly, lisping out some more information. People sometimes wondered what he said about them in other places.

'He took his time about lavin',' as the dog scurried round the side of the house again to snarl at the back wheel.

'My dear Mick and Phyllis and Rose,

I hope this letter finds you all well as it leaves us. The weather is a bit too hot at the minute. We are thinking of having a holiday this year. We will arrive at Dublin Airport on August the fifth at ten thirty. I suppose we'll get the bus then. Hope you are all well. Your loving sister, Veronica.'

Veronica. Veronica. His heart swelled up. The best of them. I wonder how long she'll be here for.

'We'll have to get some way of meeting them.'

Phyllis smiled.

'Of course, of course.'

That would be nice. A day to Dublin and then Veronica. She hadn't been here for years. He'd hate her going back but there would be the holiday first.

The excitement of getting ready for the trip created a near nauseous air in the kitchen. Rose's envy of them seeped from her pores mixing with the preparations, creating an atmosphere bigger than the three of them. If only they would go soon, she thought, get into the hired car out of sight, she would be able to be Rose again. That thought hopped from her to Phyllis and Phyllis moved to the bedroom door.

'I'll go and put on me.'

The wait at the airport was long, people and more people coming out in dribs and drabs looking exactly like Veronica but never her. People who came out expecting one or three to meet them – instead there were six.

'That looks like his brother.'

'Something the cut of your Joe.'

'A bit like stuttery Jordan too.'

They both laughed at the mention of someone not remembered for a decade. Maybe they would have liked to hold hands to calm such excitement and to mark a good day. Ah well, you can't have everything. They went quiet again and there she was, definitely. Definitely her. Check again – there had been other people. Years change faces. But no, that was her. His Veronica. Her near sister. They tried to hold back tears as they squeezed each other near to death. And the child, look how big he's got.

'Where's Roderick?' He hated the name. The question hung in the air, Veronica turned to the child. 'Philip, can you get that bag? Oh, he's not with us, and help Phyllis with that other bag.'

'It's just we thought when you said that yous were coming we thought he'd be here too.'

She might have told us. Phyllis knew first. She felt the word divorce shaping itself inside her throat. A divorced woman. A divorcee. She felt sick. The blood rushed to her head and she caught Mick's hand. Please let him say no more, let it rest. She would tell him tonight. Better still she would not tell him at all. Men should not be told these things. It would upset them too much. Neither would she tell Rose. You couldn't tell a thing like that to a child. But that's not what happened. In the scullery Mick whispered to her 'Has she told you what happened?'

His face was drawn. Rose passed the door and heard their loud frightened whispers.

'They've been apart for five years.'

'Five years. Five years. Well there's hardly any hope then.'

He came out of the scullery and nearly bumped into Rose. He didn't see her. Veronica sat in the kitchen, knowing that they were talking about her, and thought, I should never have come but Mick came past her and said we'll go up to Latton tomorrow and she said that would be lovely the child would like it, he caught her hand in a tight squeeze and in bed he said, 'Could they not have patched it up?' and Phyllis tried to repeat as faithfully as possible what his Veronica had said.

'Women are like cats. You hit them away from you and they move a little further down the couch, you hit them again they move to the next most comfortable seat. I moved from comfortable places to the next most comfortable part, moved, moved, moved until there was nowhere comfortable left to go. Then I left.'

Mick stayed quiet. This certainly wasn't the Veronica from home. She also said that the worst part was when the child's handmade Mother's Day card got mixed up with the divorce papers and she posted the card away to the court and lost it. She said that was the worst part.

'That was a funny thing to say', Mick ventured and turned his back. Phyllis turned with him and put her tissue stomach up against his still rounded bottom, rolling up her legs under his ell shape. She put her arm around his flabbing waist, he caught her fingers in a big rough well-worked hand and they thought together poor Veronica, there are things you'd miss like death.

Chapter Ten

Veronica stayed for three weeks. Phyllis thought it difficult, when she remembered, to have such a sinner in the house but surprisingly she forgot quite a bit. Veronica talked of times past and Mick encouraged. Phyllis let herself forget about evil and moved back with them as they picked over childhood happenings that had individual importance for them, the time she sold the eggs for the price of the dance, the time, the time.

'And do you remember the time?'

'God will you ever forget the time.'

All his things had got to do with work, the rain pouring on him into his skin, the hardness of a foreman, 'He knew how to crack the whip,' and later walking cattle to a fair. His sparse words, about fair mornings, drew up for Rose not cold and hunger as they were meant to but a colourful dawn, and a conspiratorial sharing of silence with semi-darkness. Instead of his famished overworked body Rose saw a secret glamour attached to the hoof clopping of cattle and him towards a still sleeping town. A chance for him or for any person to place themselves, against the sky, the countryside, others. Surely that time of morning had given him an edge on town people, but no, he recalled only hardship. He didn't remember anything to do with dances either. He did really but he left it to the women to say it, and grinned. It wasn't his place to be remembering things like that, yet why do the women always get the good parts to tell?

'And do you remember the time . . .' but that was a bad thing to bring up because it was a week before their mother had died.

'Yes I do. I do indeed.'

And so into the night.

Because Philip had to have a room of his own Veronica slept in the bed with Rose. It was not the best arrangement for a visitor, but what could they do? It suited Rose perfectly although she swallowed a lot the first night. By the second morning she and Veronica were on comfortable pillow-whispering terms, like old long-time women lovers grown into the one heart. Veronica told her about the fights with Roderick, years of shouting, broken furniture, a broken jaw. Up to the part about the broken jaw Rose was actually fascinated with the idea of people fighting like that. It was better than not noticing, she thought, with the mountainous innocence that the young can sometimes have. Part of her didn't believe anyway that men would hit women – I suppose Veronica was making it up, or no, remembering it wrong. Veronica heard herself telling this niece forgotten episodes, angles of the story that she'd never even thought of before. Rose listened uncritically, no, not just uncritically, with admiration. Rose then related the most private fantasies and disappointments of her own to this stranger, Aunt yes, but rank stranger nevertheless. In the telling of them, they became acceptable – why not? Whereas before they had smelled of odiousness. Veronica understood every word, every blunder. They each had found unexpected allies and that always made for a good day.

Veronica wasn't like other returned Yankees – she had for instance seen the Cliffs of Moher, *before* leaving Ireland. She described them to Rose, the colour, the way you understood the earth when you saw it sitting there like a sleeping dog in the sea. She painted the picture truly, so that Rose could now understand geology. What a relief for the Leaving. Philip was quiet and loved his mother, without knowing it, therefore, he liked Rose as he measured how she treated Veronica. He had a wireless called a transistor (Rose couldn't very well insist on it being called a radio because it *was* a wireless), which he carried with him everywhere, even to the shop.

'It's as small as a hair roller!'

Rose decided not to be embarrassed by this. He had however one irksome habit that she could not overlook – he would jump up and take a photograph when they or her parents or anyone, even visiting neighbours, were in the middle of a sentence. The camera sloped from his neck restlessly, waiting to interrupt the natural flow of things. At the most awkward of moments he pressed the most delicate of conversations on to film, making them tangible, remembered, and also ending them with the same gesture as the neighbours turned to eye him suspiciously. Veronica didn't like it because Mick and Phyllis didn't like it but she said nothing. He was after all her son and American. She couldn't expect him not to be American.

The days melted into each other too fast. It was strange how they could get used to anything, even a divorced woman, but Rose knew by the overheard whisperings that they were reminding themselves. She wished they'd just let it go.

'I had him sized right down to a T the first time I laid eyes on him, so I did.' 'Deed and you had.'

'I always thought a body'd be as well getting away from him as conny as they could.'

Which nearly meant that Veronica was right. Veronica walked into the room. 'Is it true that they put make-up on the corpses in America? Someone was telling me they did.'

Veronica was startled. She said 'I suppose they do,' with an edge to her voice. So after that they were more careful. If a conversation was getting too near the bone Phyllis would pat her leg and say, 'Now let me see, what'll we do for the tea.'

Veronica walked to the shop, breathing in her past and seeing her mother and father walk before her. She could hear them speak as clear as the wind. The wynd. She had said when she was nine on a threshing day, because she thought of snowflakes, 'That wynd is coming off snow.'

She had felt important saying such an adult thing that she did not understand, but immediately felt shy. They had all laughed at the old-fashionedness of her but her father had said,

'Never you mind them Veronica. They have little to be laughing at.'

He had put his hand on her shoulder, her mother had smiled, Mick had winked and tossed his head. My God would they not go away, her dead parents. The day they had sold the last of the cows she had prayed that they wouldn't take it too bad. The finishing off of a lifetime's work. In the event they hadn't looked at each other at all as he got ready for the fair, and Veronica was the one left with the lump. Her mother had said, 'well that's that I suppose' and he had said will you whisht woman can't we get more of them if we want. Such damnable unwarranted optimism put an end to the self pity that was floating around the kitchen table. Veronica could smell the guilt falling on her again, the letters she hadn't written, the one important conversation that she never had. She nipped her arm. Guilt could not be prayed away.

Kevin McGivern overtook Veronica.

'Not much hate going to loss that day.'

'Yes, it's chilly enough,' she answered grinning, delighted with herself that she had understood him so immediately and given the right answer. Long absences hadn't made her forget the language. He looked at her and said to himself, 'I'm afraid she made bad use of her time,' dismissing the whole of her life as a pointless waste of energy. She felt him thinking this and defended herself by thinking, he of the useless personality. What would he know? She shivered because in the stratification of contempt his attitude to her was about as low as you could get. Her face pinched, not knowing which way to go, at the change from her grin to her shiver, and she was glad that she was going back in three days.

At mass on the last Sunday this relief was mixed with a palpitating grief. Come on Veronica, you've lived without such love and hate before. You'll be used to your apartment in no time at all. But she was reluctant to let go of her airtight memories because they were safer than the future, naturally, being in the past. Buzzer Conlon had his young son with him, *she* mustn't be well. He tended to him as best he could, but when the child looked for a hug he blushed around his face, as if he had been assaulted. This was women's work, the hugging. Veronica watched him with as perfected a side glance as if she'd never left, and was content enough in one way to see his awkwardness because it spoke of a simpler way of doing life. Things were changing here too. A honeymoon couple had the nerve to go into the one seat. (On the men's side. It would have been too much to expect a man to move across the other way.) The two people, Veronica couldn't place them, maybe they were strangers, both had fuzzy curly hair that came six inches out from their scalps. They leaned over to say something to each other, another thing that Veronica could not remember happening before, and because of their fuzzy heads their hairs nearly touched. The sun came through the plate glass cruci-fixion window and lit on them, fusing their two heads, through their touching curls, with a shaft of blue light. Jesus, the next thing people will be kissing at mass. Veronica wandered from the back of a head to the back of another, hats, a bit of grey, a balding patch, a bad perm under a hat, collars of coats, the turning heads of impatient children who knew that they couldn't be seen, hat pins, until at last it was over and she was now set on the journey back. People shook her hand and said maybe we'll see you in a few years' time and she said next year definitely I'm coming next year I won't leave it as long again and Phyllis could feel tears coming to the back of her eyes.

The morning Veronica left, Kevin McGivern asked Mick, 'Are the holiday makers gone?' and let a long hmmmm out of him that deserved a slap in the jaw, but Mick would never do that. He didn't necessarily believe that people were entitled to such bottomless prejudice against his Veronica but he couldn't do much about it.

Rose missed Veronica like a twin and bore some resentment against Phyllis and Mick for it. (Mick had in the coming of Veronica become Mick the same way as Phyllis had become Phyllis with one photograph.) She had to resent them because there was no one else to take out her dejection on. Philip taking photos had put her off her conversation, still he hadn't mattered much, hadn't got in the way between her and Veronica. It had been a great time. It was always better to have something to miss. She would visit Veronica some day. She looked out at the yellow patch where the remains of the Austin car had been. For years she had hated it. Any time her eye fell on it, which was at least twice a month – the other thousand times she looked out the window the ruin had flown – she felt her head blowing up with madness at that oul' wreck of a thing. It had been dumped one day outside the kitchen window before Rose was born,

'Not *straight* outside the window!'

'Just for a day or two until I move it, anyway it's the back of the house', but it had never been moved because there weren't enough men around and anytime there was they were needed for something important like threshing, not making the view more pleasant. Could you imagine a woman saying to the backs of the fed hurrying thresher men after the dinner, 'Just a minute before yous go, now there's so many of yous here could yous just put your shoulders to that oul' piece of junk out there and shift it. I know yous are in a hurry but with so many of yous it won't take a minute.' Could you just imagine? Rose could, but then she was too big for her boots at times. The yellow patch looked even white sometimes against the other grass. It had yielded up twenty years of slugs and nameless creepy crawlies, parted company with whole villages of life and now lay exposed to fresh air, having nothing to fight back with except a sickening smell. But even that was going, as individual grasses went green and the wind unmatted the plaited inmates. Phyllis had said the day after the letter, 'The car'll have to be moved this time' and because it was Veronica and because there were no more excuses to hand – it was moved. So there would be a monument to Veronica – a clear piece of blessed nothingness where once there had been an eyesore. Rose looked now past the forever gone wreck to the friesian cows – a field of friesian cows. The black on one cow sometimes matched the white on another or looked as if it would fit jigsaw-like into another. That's why a field full of them always looked better than one, even if it was still an unfinished pattern. Each field of them should run into another and on and on until there would be a completed absolute shape of black and white. She let her mind dally over that until she had to ask herself 'is this all I have to think about? Friesian cows? I miss you Veronica. I miss you.'

Veronica had said 'Do you not have any particular girl-friend that you could discuss these things with?'

Girl-friend? Only boys could have girl-friends. Surely she meant friend. Yes she did have some friends, not particular ones, but she wouldn't trust them with secrets like that. She had always been alone, it was safer to stay alone, at least to keep her thoughts alone even when her body mixed with others. But Veronica was different – Rose didn't mind telling her bits and pieces of important things because Veronica understood and Veronica wasn't around now. Rose moved outside and sat in the shelter of the haystack, inhaling the few years of her history that were there. One side of the stack was cut razor-sharp with a hay knife, sometimes not in a straight line so there were steps for the fairies to walk on and indeed to hang from when the cutting jutted out instead of in. Animals and fairies. Fairies and animals. They were all right but what about other things? When was she going to see other things? Sometimes Rose thought that she would crack open for the want of knowing. Her whole body would pour out to grab some, lots, of the unknown world before going back inside her skin. Then she would be happy. Look at some of the other girls in her class – look how happy they were. Why couldn't she be like them? One of them had a continuous purple neck. Love bites, Rose was told. That was easy to follow, not like the tight camouflaged scraps in the Sunday paper that passed as information. What is a french letter? Oh God now she would know, now she would find out, once she got a chance to read the column when everyone was having their Sunday rest. It is a form of contraception. Rose flung the paper, *what* is contraception, she hissed. French letter, it must be something to do with french kissing. France was obviously the place to be. Love bites, yes. Áine with the love bites. You'd never expect a girl with a fada on her name to have love bites. Everytime one was clearing up, fading in colour, she came into school with another. Rose contemplated her, one bitten girl, one sucked girl, and got tingles in the sharp parts of her body. But yet there was something vulgar – Rose would have liked them where no one but she could see them. How daring. She smiled to herself. The class was grateful to Áine because the purple marks reminded them daily of another world, a place realer than real, that some dared to believe they would reach later. Many of the girls lapsed into daydreams looking at Áine's neck, so much so that a nun took Áine aside and dressed her down, but Áine came into school the next day with a blinder of a bite and the nun had to admit defeat. Her words against his teeth – she hadn't a hope. But she did implore Áine to think of God and Áine said that she would turn over a new leaf, that she would definitely keep her coat closed anymore on dates. Rose sighed, she knew so little – both worthwhile noble things, and low delicious things that were not low at all, really noble too, she was sure.

She got up from the shelter of the haystack because a wind had risen and she was shivering now. When she came around the corner of the house the wind had gathered up so much she had to push against it, nearly lying on it, breathing in exhilaration. Her day would come yet. She stepped into the house and lay against the door to shut the wind out. Water flowed from her eyes and nose, prickling the wind heat that had sunk inches into her face. The coal heat from the fire fought to gain control of her skin, and won as the outside elements gave way to inside comfort.

Mick and Phyllis were idly having a conversation, any conversation.

'I wonder will they put up the children's allowance in the next budget.'

'It won't make any difference to us anyway, this time.'

They smiled at Rose, she grinned back wishing she could slip away from home on words like that and not have to face the hard bits.

A certain expectancy now filled the house. The last big thing had happened before Rose would leave to do whatever it was that she would do when the results came out. Because Veronica had been here, a visit that had loosened Mick up a little, and because Rose would very soon be doing the Leaving, he manoeuvred a walk with her.

'We'll walk the length of the shop.'

Rose was startled at such a near incestuous remark from him but went out. She stood to let him through the front door before her. They walked a little and the silence grew to seventeen years in minutes of unspoken words.

'It's quite nice today.'

Her mouth was dry.

'Ay, if it holds up we'll be all right.'

He coughed.

'If we got a run of even a few days like it, we'd be away on a hack. Now when you go away your mother and me want . . .'

Want want she thought. Your mother and me want. Do you now? No sir I'll do the wanting from now on. How dare you talk to me now.

'Yes,' she said.

He knew he'd lost her but he talked on to the hedges, to the sky, to thin air. The sound of his voice pleading for some kind of order gradually softened her and she decided to forgive him certain things. Reluctantly she rolled up spiteful memories and threw them out, away. No you can't have a fringe, it looks trampish. No child of mine will be caught dead in one of them mini-skirts, they'll ruin her kidneys. Can I have beetle boots? No. Your father says that he doesn't like that pointy bra that you're wearing. These boots are made for walking and that's just what they'll do, one of these days these boots are gonna walk all over you – switch that thing off. His voice came down a notch to everyday matters, then hardened to the threats of an outside world. So your mother thought we should have this talk. What talk – I do not hear any. But the importance of the walk was not lost on Rose and she told him what she thought, really, in unspoken words. I would be your kind of good if I could but I'm promising nothing. I cannot stay here, every thought I think they search out to laugh at it. Lucky I can stay so silent or I'd be laughed dead by now. Every thought I do say, they disagree. There's them and me. I must crawl away from here so I can stand somewhere else. They do not want to know here. No not just here of course not just here, here is no worse than anywhere else but don't you see I'm known here. I can try out in other places, my life can be one big experiment. Of course that won't make me happy but I'll know, won't I? So if I have to sin I'll sin. I'll know then why the priests and you think that love is the only evil. O God help me, God help me how will I do it?

'And you'll come home as often as you can.'

'Yes of course.'

But I'll never be back here once I've left it. My spirit will go to somewhere else and then I will not be harmed. I will have a place in which to leave the raw parts of my mind, so I'll be fine, unhurtable, when I come to see you. I'll have left my thoughts behind. Oh I wish, Rose thought, looking at him, oh never mind. She wished his deafness had begun to improve sooner. Maybe if he'd heard her chattering through these years he might have understood. And how could she leave Phyllis, who yearly became more a sister than a mother? Who would go shopping now with Phyllis, feel materials, try on shoes, rub down furniture? But she had to. Her father thought, well she hasn't heard one word of that but what more can a body do. She'll have to learn. By the time they got back to the house she had forgiven him most things.

And so the spring ebbed out and summer warned of examinations. A lethargy had fallen on Rose that threatened her when she tried to cram in the essential bits of knowledge. How it would be if they were reading Mary Wollstonecraft, or Witches, or painting beach scenes. Rose you must learn you must learn, your life depends on this. But the heat came early and made her sleepier. By now she was smoking ten cigarettes a day, some of them publicly – she always smoked now after she kissed a boy and there had been four of them with, oh, it must have been one hundred kisses between them, some long gropey ones, some pretty harmless, five of them really worth waiting for and thinking about on an uneventful day. (Three times she just couldn't wash her face for a while, only once had she decided not to wash her teeth.) She was also criticising the New Mass for not going far enough while others were thinking that it was a disgrace, changing to English. If you put altar boys sitting on chairs instead of the altar steps heaven knows where it would end. Once a thing as immense as that is changed in a young person's life you make them believe that everything can change. It could be as big to one child as, say, going to Australia. And if you lose one child who's to say how many more. As well as the New Mass there was New Maths, the New Irish, and talk of New Money. Rose thought the newness was part of being seventeen.

Some days she was full of kindnesses, other days she thought venomous thoughts about perfectly mild people who on yesterdays she would have considered certainly as entitled as herself to live. Mrs Keenan sat beside Rose on the bus.

'It's great to get sittin'.'

Oh God, moaned Rose, I do not wish to get involved with a stuffy tight-lipped Pioneer like you. Mrs Keenan was elsewhere working out some terrible problem.

'God direct me,' she mumbled.

God direct you to move your arse to some other seat. Mrs Keenan was wearing a lined black-purple two-piece but the skirt must have been on crooked because the lines on coat and skirt never met no matter how she twisted or turned the top half of her body. God what an awful suit. Make you vomit, thought an uppity Rose. Mrs McKenna sat in the opposite seat. Wait until you hear them now. Two mild women being cut to bits by a Rose who had obviously had enough. She lit a cigarette, openly on the bus, put her feet up on the back of the seat, and pulled her skirt up. The two women looked at her, one joined mean look, wishing she was one of their own and they could put manners on her. Poor Phyllis. They talked then in a low pitch. They would not sully their words by letting them out loud for the like of her to hear them. Poor Phyllis indeed.

At home as the days passed they were getting nervous. The nervousness came out in begrudgement.

'Mel Traynor collects the Lindens for mass now on a Sunday and them with married sons not five miles away. You'd think Minnie would come home from Dublin and her not married. All she has up there is a job.'

'Did you take a look at the Deaths yet.'

'Poor Katie went in the end.'

Of course she went in the end. Come on, let's treat this thing seriously – she died. Do you want to talk about death? No. I thought not.

'At least the nurse said she died. But they said later that when they got her into the ambulance they found a pulse. The nurse, it seems, hoped they didn't because if they did she'd be a vegetable all her life. Well if they did it went again.'

Rose nearly cried. She never remembered them talk so much of death. Would they think of nothing now but death? Perhaps she had better not go. She could always find a job. And maybe someone to marry, later. But Phyllis shook herself. Come on Mick, we'll get used to it. Last night she had dreamt of Rose the baby, she was kissing her through a hole in a glass window. Rose then put on her coat in the distance outside a school, a secondary school, and walked over the mattress in the nursery bed in the maternity in Monaghan and kissed her back through the glass of an incubator. There she was now walking up the school yard, her coat collar half turned in, and Phyllis woke. She was glad that she had been able to love Rose as perfectly as that, in moments, because something told her it might not always be easy now. Rose looked stubborn. New Mass, the New Irish, New Money. What next? But Phyllis knew that Rose could never be evil, bad but not real evil so the best thing to do was get up, pull Mick into shape, and go visit Mrs Toal.

The morning Rose left she wore a mustard flared dress below the knee buttoned up the front with puffed-up sleeves. There was a cigarette burn on the cuff which she tried to hide from Phyllis. She was on her way to university – none of the three people here knew anything about a university, nor anyone other than a priest who had ever been there. Either God had been good or this was getting to be a great country. They all had tickles in their throats so Rose decided to think about what was in her week-end case and Phyllis ran to it an odd time to check that she had not forgotten anything. They could busy them-selves practically around this case, organising came to them as morning after sunrise. Mick, however, was at a loss. He said, half joking: 'You can't wait to get away', and when Rose tried to protest, too much no doubt, he smiled back at her. They bumped into each other a lot in that last half hour. Phyllis took a photo of Rose trying to look sombre, standing beside the week-end case. When the car came Mick (suddenly) had something to do behind the byre. Rose bit her lip most of the way to Dublin. Phyllis cried a little and then started a new life-time of too much, sometimes too little, interest in her only child's life.

Chapter Eleven

Yes, that is Rose stacking cups, cleaning the leftovers off plates with her nose turned up. She makes people despise themselves momentarily with that expression. Yes, that is Rose rubbing her legs and yawning on the 19A bus as it lurches up Phibsboro Road. Yes, that is Rose drinking too much with an altogether unsuitable man. You think he's unsuitable but Rose couldn't care less. She's drinking with him because she happened to meet him and he happened to ask and she's entitled to mindlessness like anyone else. You are annoyed – she was not supposed to end up there, what happened, you demand, so that you will know why you blame her for not being whatever it was that you wanted her to be by now.

Only Rose knows why she could not accept their way of learning. She thought it would be like Newman's *Idea of a University*, instead it was a scattered pack of cards made of concrete. When they handed out library lists she bought all the books because she thought she had to and they didn't deign to tell her otherwise. When she found this out it was the last straw. Half the time she had not understood a word anyway. They all spoke with English accents. Or so she thought. This was no place for her. No one would care that she, Rose, was collapsing in on herself daily. And still no Salem Witch Trials. Other girls had sisters in flats and jobs to make sure that their clothes would not let them down, or better still they lived at home. People knew people, knew where buses went to and came from, had so much money, had passed the building so often that it was just a building, a place they naturally went to after school. No, this

123

was no place for her. Rose closed down hope and ran out the glass door, as yet too stung to know what or why.

She got a job, a little waitressing, a little dishwashing, and tried hard to forget that she had nearly got a university education. The means of forgetting were sometimes light-hearted, sometimes squalid.

Rose had found a trustworthy, witty flatmate. She had expected to and didn't know yet that she had in fact been lucky. She met Dymphna in the hostel, which had been a cross between a convent, a hospital, a jail and a school for sex. The loudest talk was of going matters – going out with, going to bed, going steady, boys going with boys, girls going with girls – and people who knew such people, girls who had been gone on Sister so-and-so – and for relief, going home. The walls were tired of the same yearly confidences, while inmates believed completely in their own originality. They had come to Dublin among the general flurry of school leavers, the boys with new suits, the girls with black skirts and seldom carried handbags. The hat and gloves only proved now that your mother wasn't moving with the times. The ones who were not going to university concentrated on appearance for the interview, little knowing that the interviewers would be too old to know what was fashionable. But they got their jobs anyway and passed through the hostel on their way to more appropriate, comfortable, private, grown-up accommodation. Rose kept her lips closed, but behind them her mouth was open and her throat dry.

Dymphna was the middle child in a family of nine. Her mother kept meaning to put manners on her but every time she thought of it she was too tired, the lids were falling down over her eyes and she couldn't actually see the child who badly needed a slap. By looking at the others Dymphna had learned what was right and wrong, or rather what made one popular, so she was a well-mannered but unscolded free soul. Rose and she were put in the cubicles next to each other. The first night they talked into the morning, of their mothers, it seemed the natural thing to do. They told their tales jumpily, moving from unconnected things to some other private memory. They were too young and too relieved with freedom, for these memories to be hurtful. Dymphna told of how her mother would go into a tizzy every time a man came to work around the house.

'They're all right,' my mother says. 'They're great, in fact. Put a new window in for you and then ruin it, I mean ruin it with paint.'

'Sometimes she annoys me though.' Dymphna grimaced.

Dymphna's mother had told her once about fixing their friendly neighbour up for a date with a distant relation. Dymphna, unusually, had turned nasty. You're matchmaking, she spat, as if that was the dirtiest thing she could imagine. The mother thought, I should not have told her, she's too young to understand. 'She thinks there's nothing in life but getting married.'

Rose thought that her friend had certainly noticed a lot more about her mother than she had about Phyllis. There seemed to be disadvantages to large families. There would surely be too much noise to think, as there was now. There was also a lot of blackmailing.

'My sister said that if I ever caused any trouble she would tell about me seeing my Auntie Mary breast feeding.'

Rose gulped. What a way to treat a piece of knowledge.

'Mind you I was going to tell what had happened between her and James Connolly.' The happening between her and James Connolly was innocent enough although ridden of course with a power that James had not collected yet. He had said, 'Come here till I show you what I've got.'

He was delighted with himself. Dymphna's sister looked at him. It didn't excite her at all. It never even struck her that it was supposed to. In fact she didn't even look at IT – she was just aware of him wee-weeing, while thinking that she was getting too old to still use that word.

'You durty thing,' she had said, and turned her back and nearly split her sides laughing and then foolishly went home and told Dymphna.

Dymphna talked a lot, there were many superfluous words in every sentence, but that suited Rose. It created a camouflage for her as she floundered through disappointment. They got a flat together on an autumn evening. The leaves were trickling from trees and the evenings were getting darker but that was no worry to them because it would mean that there would be more of night-time and night-time was when things happened. The sitting room had a fire, the beds were clean and two feet apart, there was no clothes-line and the landlord lived downstairs. The landlady read books with Wife in the title, *The Doctor's Wife*, *The Ambassador's Wife*, *The Wife of Mr Archer the Explorer*. Those books were scattered all over the house, even in the bathroom. She had four children, all replicas of the landlord. There was a coin box phone outside the landlord's sitting room so you couldn't have a private conversation. Rose's seclusions were being chipped.

Rose threw herself enthusiastically into a life of packaged foods. It was a relief not to have to eat properly, but why then did she sometimes smell stew or Phyllis' soup? Was she just another forever child remembering her mother for comfort? It was another night and nothing particular had happened. But then the next morning she would walk out of her door and there were still hundreds of unknown people on the street, just like yesterday. There was noise and people moving fast, buses, and dancehalls that she could go to without asking permission. Towards week's end Rose and Dymphna edged their ways into a parentless social life. On a night when one of them was wary the other didn't hesitate. Their life had no clock except for the alarm in the morning. Their life had rice pudding at 3.00 am if so desired. Their life had men. Different ones. In time their lives had groping sessions, vulgar kissing and rubbing. Very occasionally their lives had a comfortable kiss or two. They got ready to go out whenever they pleased. Rose sometimes absentmindedly licked her fingers and rubbed them over her eyebrows, then licked her salty fingers. What did all this getting ready mean? An innocence. An optimism. An absolute belief in the unknown life to be led. An empty consequence of Western Romantic fiction that left rumblings in the pit of her stomach. Dymphna plucked Rose's eyebrows.

The first time Rose came home with some unknown man she willingly thought, now I can practise. Practise what she didn't know, maybe pretending that she was older than she was. She would practise looseness, pick up understanding of all that past innuendo. She had not had time for this before. For months it lasted, this wasteland of foolish mortification, the seeing of themselves, their actual being indeed, dependent on grubby compliments from nervous strangers.

Rose lined up with brave women who, as in a ridiculous farce, pretended anything that they thought was demanded of them. These women would even pretend that they were, say, nervous, when they were in fact fearless as wildcats, but shrieks of fear might get someone's attention. And worse too, than just being nervous. In time they would forget what fools they'd made of themselves. She lined up with them but never quite believed that they meant any of it.

Dymphna brought home a blond beautiful man, with wavy hair, the best looking of any they'd seen so far. He couldn't have his way with her so he came back out to the car licking his lips, proclaiming 'Jesus, the sexiest thing since the hairy ha'penny.'

Rose was still in the car, trying to discuss 'something or other' with a reluctant bus conductor who was beginning to twitch with impatience. Rose brought home a black-haired man, much older, who made her feel as if she was still in school uniform. But he knew something more than these petty distractions and only pecked her on the cheek. For that she would have done anything with him. He asked her absentmindedly what she thought of bra-burning. Rose was flustered but said she agreed, why shouldn't she – men didn't wear jock straps. And she did agree.

'Ah but there's not as much dangling going on with us,' he said seriously. 'I nearly died,' Rose told Dymphna later.

But she got over it because she knew that these embarrassments were necessary dues to the kind of adult world she hoped to inhabit.

They got ready again for the Revolution Club. Rose was wearing tearproof mascara now, why tearproof she couldn't fathom, she had no intention of crying, but she supposed it might rain. She liked to be ready before going anywhere – she disliked the lines of women doing themselves up at the mirror in whatever place they went. One woman, always here (it was not a good idea to be always here. It proved anxiousness. Cool was what got you a man) battered the make-up on as if she disliked her own face enormously. Rose felt uneasy watching, even glimpsing unavoidably, such self-disgust. But she swallowed her uneasiness. The music was reported to be the loudest in town, the place was dark, this was surely up to some standard, but Rose was bored to near weakness. She had spent too long seeking purely carnal knowledge. If it had been mixed in with other things perhaps – but all Dymphna and she had done these past few months was look at and talk of men.

The following week she met her school friend. He was up doing an interview. She had not seen him since she was eleven and it was strange to watch him now here in this place, not standing reading Irish lessons, or screaking chalk on the blackboard. They walked home together, naturally. Rose remembered the book and smarted, but when they stopped beside the sleeping watchman's hut to warm their hands he kissed her lightly as if asking for forgiveness. It was a contemplative kiss, more like a person putting their own finger on their lips and it was obvious that there was no point in pursuing it. It was then that the flutter of wonder went up from Rose to the sky, muttering 'I was right, I was right'. (More extraordinary, she was still to think that twenty years from now, but by then she knew that it was simply the unattainable preciousness attached to the now, forever comparative, impossible innocence.) She was in fact embarrassed by such a beautiful kiss but then thought who the hell was he to embarrass her. He had turned out (Rose believed that they had reached the point where you could say that they had turned out) more shy than she, light years behind her despite, or because of, his picture books. This realisation made Rose sexually bold, or rather mentally bold, but all she could do about that was prove it in the sexual games that were being played – so the next time

128

she was at the Revolution Club she did the asking. It gave her a thunderous feeling in the middle of her stomach but when admired for her nerve she pretended, and said, blasé, 'it *is* the Revolution Club.'

Secretly she was delighted with herself. No one refused.

Dymphna was bringing home another man, by now they were losing count. When they reached his car it was full of men. Harmless men. Dymphna and Rose did indeed have an enormous amount of luck, considering some of the strange men they could have met. They – the men – just told each other jokes on the way home. This second-hand litanising was not just a competition but a gap filler when they ran out of things to say. Little set pieces that had nothing to do with the larger human orchestra of humour. Rose looked out the window, quiet, unmoved and vaguely aggravated. Then the car broke down. The young men peered into the bonnet, Rose and Dymphna stood on the footpath.

'If we gave her a push', but the push didn't work. 'Maybe she's out of petrol.' No, not possible.

The one who knew the mechanical suggestions was rising rapidly in all their estimations, but when would he hit on the right thing?

'When did you last have her serviced?'

'Perhaps if you tried calling *it* "him" *it* might go of its own accord,' Rose said in a premeditated way. Her voice came cold through the air, an unnecessary slap, upsetting the balance, sounding ungrateful. It was after all they who were trying to fix the car. Bad timing for demanding rights. Weren't they, the two of them standing there on the footpath looking pretty and useless (never mind that three of the men knew nothing about engines either), weren't they the two of them getting respect? Wasn't that enough? The men got the car going and brought them home. Even to the door, despite the complaining of that frosty looking one. One of them, Tom, asked Rose for a date. He thought if there was a girl around, any girl even that one, and seeing it was the time of the night for date-making, he might as well, but she said 'no thank you, I'm going to join a convent next weekend so I'll be busy'. He said Ah yes. I thought you must be thinking of something serious, you were so quiet. Rose went to sleep wondering if indeed convents were full because of jokes and broken-down cars.

She munched toast in the morning as if she were on her own. Dymphna chattered on about this one and that one or was he the one who said, but Rose had retreated. The rituals were exhausting her. True, she was teething with freedom, and within that teething anything was acceptable. She hadn't deliberately set out to rid herself of innocence but rather to collect evidence of life, yet how was she to know what kind of life this one was? What did she have to compare it with? There had to be more than kissing men. She'd never have time to read again if this thing kept up. She had met only one, one only, man who knew anything equal to or more than her. The black-haired man. Now he would have been all right but he hadn't liked her, Rose thought. (In truth, he would have and could have made the most mature love yet to her, but he hesitated. He knew that someone else would do it, probably not as well as him, but he didn't want to break the trust she had set up with her dreamy beliefs. She said that a book was placeless. Whether you read it in New York or Kabul or Navan it was the same book. His eyes opened at that – a surprised hurt kind of look at such observance. Would it be wasted? He should see this young woman again, but he accepted that people like him, and she was too but didn't know it yet, never managed to hold on to the suitable people. Born losers every way except in their heads. Ah – someone else would make love to her, because she would want to find that out too, someone smart enough to get her attention and probably weak enough to drain her with his own lesser importance.)

She made herself another slice of toast. During these unashamed cheap few months at least she hadn't had to worry about her reputation like she would have had to do at home. That was something, and she had some important observations. She smiled. A twingey Phyllis kind of smile. She had never looked more like her mother. On her way to work she caught sight of a dark, fine, man working down a hole in the street. He gazed at her, stripping her with his look. She looked away, feeling nervous in the face of such presumption. He snarled at her as she passed, 'You'd look at me, you bitch, if I had a suit on.' She was startled by the truth of this, and frightened by his viciousness. She quickened her step. All day she thought of the sinister side of that man. In her nightly meetings with strangers was she in fact playing with something more dangerous than each individual one of them – the wider field of men? Was this indeed why marriage was a good idea? Funny how men seldom whistled after another man's ringed woman.

She gave up the Revolution Club and set about getting a real job. – Real? How dare you be so disloyal to the too skinny or the too fat who have slogged with you these last few months? In truth she was sacked. Waitresses should know the difference between men and women customers. Men have to be pampered lightly, and titillated a little, just a little. Women are customers who are not men, you expect them to stack their saucers and plates. A man customer complained to Rose five times during his meal; she dropped the teapot on his table, from one and a half feet up, scalding the tip of his finger ever so slightly, and screamed 'Pity you didn't bring your own nanny with you.'

A loyal and expectant silence fell down over the café, while they got her wages ready. The other waitresses smiled edgily, not wishing to complicitise.

The office job was colder. The office girls were mostly scared, except for one who talked always in the toilet of how 'people should express their feelings'. The secretaries arched their foreheads at that. Rose lowered her eyes when passing the navy-jacketed, grey-trousered automatic men. Her boss had a lopsided grin, he said he loved to see women walking down Grafton Street without bras. That tore Rose between wanting to burn with the best of them and not wanting to satisfy his lunch-time ogling.

The office job meant that Phyllis could be asked to visit. She came with brown bread, scones, rhubarb, cabbage, broad beans and a few decent potatoes. She liked the flat but was shy of

Dymphna. She did not ask Rose about her new job, thus treating it with as much contempt as the last one. Rose bristled a little at the forlorn look she pulled down over her face when work was mentioned. Phyllis sat down beside the fire, lost for something to do. She had never ordered her daughter about, she had asked her to do things, she had even said please and thanks long before people started being nice to their children. Perhaps she should have laid down the law. Perhaps, perhaps. She was knotted up with disappointment yet a little pleased at the confidence of Rose. Where could she have got that from? Luckily she didn't guess that some of it came from having men's trousers up against the inside of her thighs. That would naturally have appalled her. Some women, men, and mothers should never be told these things because they abuse the preciousness of confidences like these. They make them into stories, or tragedies, or moral issues, when they should be kept as accidental intercourses.

When Dymphna's mother had come there had been terrific bustle. She had passed through busily. Rose barely had time to think, so this is Dymphna's mother, peach-quiet lipstick, so peach you could almost smell it – you certainly couldn't take your eyes off it – but so quiet nevertheless that it was inoffensive. Contrary to what the lipstick suggested, the wearer wrung the minutes dry in Dublin, going back dizzy with shopping and the picture they had seen, *Madame X*. Phyllis, in contrast, came apologetically and waited by the fire. The visit could have been a disaster, the silences could have built into a big flood, but the Saturday evening meal out cancelled temporarily all accusations. This was how it would be for now, between Rose and Phyllis – balancing act of guilt, accusation, and loyalty. Rose didn't take Phyllis for a meal out, she went with her which is what made the difference.

They sat at the table unfussily. Phyllis was a noticeable woman, long, with a strikingly content face. She had come to terms early with her only average looks.

'That looks terrific on you,' never 'you look terrific'.

The garment always got the commendation, not Phyllis. But because she had accepted this before she was thirty, a twinkly sort of confidence accompanied her. As well as that her face was wearing well, and she didn't have to worry about fat. They studied the menu together, mumbling.

'That would be nice.'

'No, not with that though.'

'Oh, with that. Yes with that.'

Rose had watched another girl her age taking her mother here. The girl had ordered for her mother in a loud stroppy voice, the mother had looked out the window ashamed at such a thoughtless know-all. Rose had thought 'How thoroughly unkind. And obvious. And uncalled for.'

Everything that girl had done that day, Rose did not do today. They commented on the food, whispered about the people who passed their table, and counted out the bill between them. Phyllis said, 'Are you coming home next week-end?'

And it was the right moment.

'Yes. Oh, yes,' Rose said, smelling grass and real soup. After mass on Sunday, (Rose went too, afraid to say what freedom she had found burrowing her way out from under Jansen) Phyllis sighed, 'That's that over' as if she hadn't depended on it. But in a way this mass was not as important as the one at home. Here could never be as important as that. Phyllis left the dinner, taking with her promises, home, and Rose's nineteen years. Rose cried a little with longing and also with some relief.

And so they, Rose and Phyllis, spent the next six months purling in and out of each other's lives, being sometimes all open wound, other times careful. Rose went home – a spectator to her past life – and left at week-end's end relieved but also, she had to concede, resuscitated by such endlessness. Once she brought Dymphna with her but their quiet house, their three solitary lives, recoiled from her noisiness and went silent. For a minute Dymphna thought they were all a bit strange, but only for a minute because Dymphna couldn't sustain thought too long – it interfered with speech.

The following week-end Dymphna went to her own home and Rose was alone in their flat, where she dreamt of an interesting man – he rubbed her back and talked of interesting things. Then he lifted her up like a child and put her sitting on his hip bone where she could feel lovely and warm. As she woke, she rubbed the last bit out because this was just her getting side-tracked again. She tried to put him together. Interesting? How interesting? What made him interesting? Rose, what do you mean by interesting? Oh you know, reads books, is different, that sort of thing. Richish, just for a change. Rose wished she could stop thinking about men – they were no good for her. That was not what she wanted to do. Look at men. They moved about and learned things, women sat down and talked about babies – having them, how many, what age, not having them, how not to have them, never having them, sterilisation, what if you changed your mind. Oh but well yes, she conceded, but I want to do both. I think I want to learn things but I most certainly do not want to be a man. The second night she went to bed early with three books. That would banish these pointless longings.

She fell asleep in her contented place where there was no death and lots to do in the morning. She was woken by screams, terrified crying. She jumped from her bed, ran downstairs to the landlady. The landlady would do for a mother, protector. The screams got louder, piercing yelps, eerie unhuman pleadings. They came from the landlady's bedroom. They came from the landlady. Rose shouted. 'Are you all right?' 'Yes,' the landlady whispered back. 'Yes Rose, go to bed I was just having a nightmare.' And Rose went to bed reluctant, not wanting to believe what she had just heard, the screams of a grown woman being walloped. She felt more pity the next morning as she saw the landlady smile, smile and smile again at her, Rose, at her children, at the postman. She was glad when Dymphna came back. She said nothing. But silence was beginning to appear dangerous to her.

They settled back into using each other as buffer and tester, teasing or pushing the other out front first, never speaking a word of what was indeed love, and truer for not being understood. They didn't destroy the feeling by mentioning it.

But Rose eventually said, thinking of all that Dymphna needed to say, 'Perhaps we should get someone else in . . . then we wouldn't get too dependent on each other,' and Dymphna agreed.

Chapter Twelve

Rose sometimes feared the shocks that she got in this first year, the facts worthy of newspapers that were happening to people to whom she had actually spoken in the flesh, – unmarried motherhood, a sister separated, a riot in the north. Who could the rioters be? But the fear didn't stop her. She collected more and more crimes against humanity, mostly against women, not realising that she was putting the world on trial. She thought that she was just noticing and drawing obvious conclusions. The end verdict of the relentless questioning of such ordinary people could be that neither she nor anyone else had any cause to satisfy general morals. The morals were those of a sneaky bunch of men who had always been old. Young fearless people were saying – we will have it our way, there is a new road, an open order. (Open until they would be thirty-five and afraid of depressed eighteen-year-olds.) Rose slid into the new order practically overnight, after she heard the landlady screaming. It was easy. Weren't nuns leaving convents in their droves? She decided to attend a political meeting. She saw the notice and found the address but she could not understand all of what they said and they seemed strangely controlled. They talked a lot of standing orders, motions, points of information. Through the chairman please – for what earthly reason? She would try somewhere else. The next week she had found two posters. If she had gone to the other one she would have been saved a lot of trouble.

The day before she went to this meeting was a definite spring day. Spring crept up on a city – it took a long time to notice burrs oozing sap. But that early morning she had heard a bird singing in the lightening blackness, one bird teasing both the dark and her. Tweet. Long silence. That could not have been a bird. Tweet. It was. Silence. Tweet, tweet, tweet. Fingers would never tease Rose like a bird. And the sun had kept up all day, changing colours through her office window, giving people colds because they threw off their big jumpers in a mischievous fling, at one in their gesture with the jumping new lambs. Mick would be looking out over the fields. Phyllis would be getting into good form. Rose went to the meeting that night.

The man visually expressed an interest in her. Three times, during the serious matter of the political consequences of the North, the EEC, and contraception. She was glad that he didn't look at her during the short debate on contraception. It was he who talked about it, saying women needed it. There was a resigned nervousness about the group, they couldn't call themselves what they called themselves if they didn't discuss this matter but oh the shame of it. The barman looked threateningly over. The EEC was easier. Rose didn't look at him because this man was, well, above her, really. A man who knew everything that confused her. But he got on the same bus as her and sat down beside her and talked to her and made a date. Well not a date exactly –

'I'd like to meet to discuss that. Are you free, let me see, next Tuesday – no Wednesday?'

'Yes,' rushed Rose like a fool.

She should have thought for a minute first. But how could she think. She was being offered a date with a communist. Wednesday then. And it wouldn't be pathetic or vulgar. It would be pure.

The rest was blur. Moss. His face, his wrist, his eyes – two of them – became what love meant. His name. Moss. Moss, heather and kisses. His watch with a black face. The hair on his wrist under the watch. Time, daylight, other people, flowers coming out, lights winking in the rain, darkness, books, even bookshops, songs, every song ever written, all became credits of their love. Moss and Rose. Rose and Moss. She could not believe

137

that she had ever been so good to deserve such triumph over the ordinary. Each day was a personal glory. Imagine, nothing could make this not last forever. It would be a pleasure to die after a life like this. The happiness was merciless. Rose was more impatient than Moss, she lost her head quicker, she was more willing to throw the whole lot into this violet coloured bubble. She understood reluctantly that he would of course have to reserve parts of himself for outside this love. He had after all serious political commitments. You could not grin widely while discussing the *whole* world. This was the cause for more infatuation on her part, how could he switch off like that? If she had to speak in the same room as him she would probably titter with happiness and make a fool of herself and him. Wasn't he marvellous. Just marvellous. She started thinking 'fabulous' and even 'fantastic'. Before, these words had embarrassed her. But now she was ready. She would learn from him, too.

Once she put her hand on his shirt where his heart was and felt it beat below her fingertips. Ticking, ticking, living. How could such a perfect person be. And she had met him and he loved her. He asked her the time, because his watch, with the black face, was being fixed. She lied so that he would miss his bus and they could kiss for longer. He would thank her and love her the more because she wanted him so much. He could get a taxi later. But when in fifteen minutes the church clock rang the exact time, he frowned, annoyed. He seemed to suspect her. She was frightened by his look of irritation. When he left she put it to the back of her mind because he had after all kissed her again. She slept with her fingertips touching the sheet lightly, as if his heart beating was under it. But two days later he hadn't rung. The panic came over Rose in waves –

'Jesus you shouldn't have,' she snapped at Dymphna who had rung her at work, 'Don't you know I'm expecting Moss. You put the heart crossways in me.'

Dymphna said sorry but meant dear me. Dear me. Rose said sorry, sorry and Dymphna said it's ok, it's ok and meant it in a flush of sympathy. Rose thought I will have to ring him. I will have to find some way. I know that he would agree that I should take some initiative because he does believe that women are equal. But how can I, how could I, I've never done it before. It will look obvious. Oh God in heaven but I have to. That's it . . . my book. I forgot my book and there's an address written on it. Casual, casual. But why couldn't I wait? No, no I'll get sick if I wait. Six, seven, two, eight, three, four, – what a beautiful number. Ring, ring, ring. Hello, it's Rose, it's just that I forgot my book in your flat . . . He was friendly. He would ask her out tomorrow. Warm, warm Rose.

'I'm going to Moscow tomorrow, for a week.'

'Gosh that's lovely.'

'I'll post the book and I'll see you when I get back. Thursday, let me see, the eighteenth then. Lovely. Bye.'

That's that then. How could she ever be good enough for a man who is going to Moscow. But he brought her back poems by Pushkin and she tried to look into his face, but it was hard because she got sunstruck.

Moss was in love too. But his mother hadn't hugged him much. His father hadn't hugged him at all. His father had never hugged his mother. He didn't know much about love and Rose didn't know that. He never told Rose that he loved her, in fact he told her that love was a proprietorial, meaningless word and Rose agreed. He asked her to meet his sister, well not exactly.

'I have to meet Christina, that's my sister, and her boyfriend at eight o'clock in Rice's pub. I could meet you there too.'

If only he'd wanted her to meet them. But she scolded herself for being unreasonable. Rice's, that would be another place she could think of. The places she met him became monuments in their history, little stone places in a rock memorial, became also grand excitements stuck somewhere in her gut. She could now pass several streets and look down them and see a pub they'd sat in and remember what he'd said to her there. She sometimes even remembered what she said in reply. It made Dublin tender for her. And his sister obviously admired him, which was only right. Her boyfriend was a student. He was doing the same subjects that Rose should have been doing. It's too late, Rose. Why does it have to be too late so soon? Rice's was a dark pub with a confident centre floor running into whispering corners. The ladies' toilets were away upstairs which meant you had time to think on your way there and time to long to be back beside him, on your way back. On the way home he gave her a Christmas present. Only he could have found such a present, a dark picture of a woman looking far away (he thought she'd like a picture of a woman) and a yellow picture of a café. Paris he said, as if she didn't know. She didn't. People talked at the tables. A woman sat being just a lovely woman. But maybe she had something to say if she was with them?

'I don't of course believe in Christmas.'

How right he is. So now everything was for her how right he is. She had not known that there were so many things not to believe in and to disagree with. Maybe to think about, and to wonder about, but to disagree with them all. How right he is. He had to be because he knew more than her, so far, and he might be a way out. She loved him. What next?

Getting Rose into bed was difficult. But Moss could do it. Rose did want it too but would not, could not have the nerve. How could she. For all her talk, no thoughts, she was reluctant to go the Whole Way. And all it needed was another person. Not any old person of course. Moss. He didn't ring again for three days. It was a good time to push his advantage. He also told her about the illnesses that sexual frustration caused in men. Gosh, she hadn't known that. There was so much she didn't know. He asked her to hold him, no, this way. Such an unsubtle rising thing. It must be an embarrassment. But she loved him in so far as she knew what that meant and he loved her in so far as he was able. So she allowed him to lead her to his bed and let herself believe that her reluctance was only natural, that the dry searing in her would have happened no matter who was inside her. She made herself forget that a kiss had once melted more silver through her. She pulled the sheets up around her neck and afterwards wondered should she offer to have them cleaned.

That was accomplished. They could now get on with what they believed they deserved. An adult life. They could talk

140

about ordinary things while all the time knowing that there was such a thing as the extraordinary. And *that* simply wonderfully because of just another person. Rose began to enjoy some of it too, although she often felt that it had little to do with her.

Saturdays became cradle time. Rose lay in bed, beaming, even with the disappointment. It was as if she were nine again. In bed sick on a Tuesday and after tea and toast Phyllis had given her two new comics, at the same moment as Mental Arithmetic was starting in school. Phyllis. Phyllis. Had she ever been this happy, Rose wondered. Moss thought that a strange thing to be thinking about at a time like this. He was fascinated, 'really amazed,' by the darkness of her pubic hair. He went on about it so much she'd swear he had been wondering about it. It was however a relief not to have him going on about her insides, or how her breasts were such a perfect handful. She smiled. How little she had to complain about. She became corrupted by his love for her body, but it was a corruption that didn't do anyone any harm because it merely made her silent, broody, and somewhat sad. Could this be everything, such love, such devotion, could this be absolutely all? Time to get up.

The accidental pregnancy was nearly inevitable. Rose was more sick than worried. She was too young to be shocked. We'll have to get married I suppose – no, no Rose, not like that. She was practising before herself. Moss had not mentioned anything and it was two weeks ago now since she'd told him. We could get married, I suppose. Shrug your shoulders, Rose. And laugh. We could get married, I suppose. Up at the end of the sentence – makes it a question mark. What a terrible thing to do to him, he who did not believe in marriage. When she said it, it was a dim sort of moment, misty enough she hoped to make her words casual. She would remember that she had had to say it. He said I suppose we could and smiled as best as he was able.

Phyllis bit her lip and worried. Mick didn't know what to think. Dymphna remembered Rose saying 'A wife. What's a wife? An ambassador. She'd have to know everything about somebody else and think always of what they were and always put their point of view. How could I do that? I don't even know myself. Yet.'

Dymphna had marvelled at such a way with words but thought she could be a wife herself rightly without any bother. What an ambassador Moss now has, she thought looking at Rose. Rose would have been annoyed if she'd known what Dymphna was thinking. That conversation was not for this room. She had enough problems at the moment.

In her home she tried not to let Moss talk too much. He would upset Phyllis with those wonderful ideas of his. It was easy for Rose, this managing of conversation. She knew the two sides, what they thought, what would upset them. She could veer them down other roads without them ever knowing that they had been diverted. It all went smoothly. She sighed with relief and yawned, exhausted.

Now Moss' mother was another story. Rose went, prepared to like her, full of curiosity, hoping to be liked herself but Mrs Brady wasn't there at all. There was a person calling herself Mrs Brady but the eyes out of Mrs Brady's face belonged to someone else. She was not interested in who her son was marrying. Her son had turned into a communist, what would she want having anything to do with him. Not interested, at all. Mind you he was no worse than the rest of them. Her grown children had all done a terrible thing to her. They were not interested in her pains. They felt that she should discuss them with her husband. But she couldn't do that. Hadn't she had children so as not to have to do that? She wanted them to save her from him and hated them because they wouldn't have anything to do with it. She tried manipulation, in the devious way that was the only one she knew. It didn't work. The grown children had got married, simply to protect themselves against their endless needs. And when that failed they had children to protect themselves. A communist. Why should she concern herself about who he was marrying. Perhaps she could have forgiven him his communism if he'd done something for her but no. Rose was prepared to try, to prove to her that yes she was the right person for her son but Mrs Brady couldn't have cared less. A communist, not a son.

The wedding was an unwanted thing. No one smiled much and Rose thought, oh my God they think they've got me now, I will have to go to university again or something or they will have got me. Is it really too late to make my claim? It was the whole world against her at the altar rails, she forgot to think about Moss. Moss thought, how did I let myself get into this, there is no need for marriage. He forgot to think about Rose. They didn't look at each other all day. They went on a short honeymoon which he called a holiday because he unbelieved in honeymoons as well and Rose had to unbelieve with him or they would have fought and she was frightened of them fighting. My wife Rose, he whispered aloud bitterly but the words didn't upset her because that wasn't her. She couldn't be anyone's wife. It was someone else who had got married this morning, it never was her. He suggested that they continue living in separate places. There was no need for them to live together just because they'd got married. They should have done it long ago, but now because of this they would leave it for some time. It would prove a point. Do you understand? That hurt. But he was fond of himself too and Rose, so she did move into his place – she told herself that he'd only said that for the sake of discussion, in case she was finding it difficult. He was so thoughtful really, behind all those necessary principles. She felt sparse in his flat. He had the accoutrements of a man going somewhere, folders, cut out papers, paper clips, an umbrella, a typewriter. There wasn't much room for her things. The only clothes of hers he liked were her knickers. Rose's hands hung loose beside her sides and bile rose in her stomach. And she began to rebel. Who wouldn't?

Surprisingly Moss got over the wedding in a few weeks. It had after all not been too hard on him at all. He had not lost much. But the toll was mounting up on Rose's face. First she filled in some forms and they asked her what her husband did. When she tried to tell them also what she did the man said it didn't matter. It didn't matter. Phyllis would like that. Then a letter came to a Mrs Moss Brady. Moss said open it, it's for you. But that couldn't be for her. That was not her name. Her fingers picked at it. It was from Phyllis. Oh well, how was she to know? Or was she? Mother I will stand here, Mothers we will stand here, while you stab us in the back.

'What's wrong with you, Rose?'

'Nothing. Must be the baby.'

She sometimes forgot about that end of things.

The Mis came in the middle of the night. The giving up of the ghost of a child. It gave up the ghost. It removed itself from Rose's young insides in a gesture of contempt at the married grown-up humans. It said I do not want to be. What a charade on my part. What a pity. Rose cried because in its leaving she realised finally that it had in fact been there. It was not all imagination. She would have dressed it in yellow, not pink or blue. Moss put his arms around her and said absentmindedly, you'll be ok. Take a long rest now. The ghost was laughing at him. Phyllis said, oh my God no, oh my good God no, and wished of all things that she liked Moss more. Mick said nothing. Rose came home bled out and bought herself a new skirt, a flecked purple wool with a hidden pleat that smelled of sickness and failure. Eventually she burned it.

What did happen between Moss and Rose to send them cold shouldering distance between each other in opposite directions? People could look at them, people did, and say well, I cannot imagine why. No one, least of all Rose and Moss, knew although Rose had unmentioned suspicions. But there was a ghost between them and they became two ghosts themselves, eating breakfast at the same table and trying not to meet alone in the evening. No strangulated hate grew up, but they began to dismiss each other. The always unfinished clash hung about the flat, and finally the bed, the war between the private Rose and the public Moss. His friends came in for tea. Always it was the same – she is curious about them, they about her but as time wears on and her need for privacy manifests itself in uneasiness, all but the oldest thinks, 'We were wrong. She's really a bit of a targe.' As she felt their interest waning she became better – now she could withdraw and with her withdrawal Moss could then shine again. Her thoughts would come up with something that made her angry and she would add a few more wicked sentences to the evening. They would look at her thinking look *dear* it's not our faults. Why did they have to be so worried? Could they not see that she was talking to herself? Then withdraw again. Moss to shine again. Will they never go home? Can they not see I live here too? No. So she would excuse herself and go to a cold bed. She would put the book under the pillow and close her eyes when she heard them leaving.

Oh to be. . . .

I wish. . . .

Rose wished brothers, sisters, a father who would have sung, a young husband who would have believed in roses. She woke up one night to the sound of Moss crying. She was shocked. She knows that she is relieved to cry – it makes her feel well. It's good that he can cry, all that pent-up emotion flowing out of him the natural way that has been denied men. It is good. She sees the small boy at the snowball fight who was booed because he cried, hatred flashing in his eyes and in his disappearing pout. Yes, it is good that men cry. But what is she to do? What is so wrong? She pretended not to hear but she did try harder for a few weeks. But try harder at what? What way she asked herself all day now, every day.

'You know the pit you get in your stomach,' she said one evening confidently. 'What pit? No I don't,' he said in the voice of a man who had been let down. 'You think I know everything that you know. You seem to think that because you know it, it is universal.'

'I only meant that I was wondering about us and just that I was thinking today, only today that we're not getting on very well.'

'What do you mean?'

'Well . . .'

The door bell rang. Moss got up and went downstairs, his jaunty steps accusing her. Rose banged the table with her fist. But there was no one there to see her, and if there had been they wouldn't have had much to say and would probably have shrugged.

They staggered through another month that had two or three good minutes in it but they were too young for that to be enough. Rose was happy *sometimes*, pleased with herself. She knew dozens of names on the library shelves and how to find more, had learned to swim, and she'd had sex, wasn't that good really. There were times that she felt like putting her arms around herself and saying you're great, she thought Moss felt like that too but he wasn't even thinking of her anymore. Other things yes but not that. Yes, he had been in love but he presumed that the new world meant that you didn't have to repeat this over and over again in tenderness. Sex was the way you showed love. He had proven all that way. Why, he had got books on different positions. He had been good to Rose – he suggested to her that she get on top, she would never have thought of that herself. The first time he brought a book out of the new paper bag Rose was made weak at such intimacy. Doing it was one thing, you got carried away and couldn't help it, you loved it, but reading about doing it with the person you were going to do it with. No. No, she thought, that's embarrassing. If only she'd been in school and not married she could have handed him back his books. She gave him a novel to read. It would be good for them to have something to share. But it took him too long to finish and then they fought about whether Ann in the book was right or not. They fought for one and a half hours over it, leaving rooms, banging doors, coming back into rooms, following each other to the bathroom. Bourgeois shit he said. Dead right she said.

'Dead right.'

'Is this a book,' he screamed, 'or real people?'

'Same thing,' she said.

'Same thing, same thing,' she roared.

'How could it be the same thing?' he said in genuine disbelief and defeat.

'I like the public thing about books. People live out their private lives on the pages. It means we can peep in at them.

146

They allow themselves to be judged and learned from. I like that nerve. I remember one time Phyllis heard a woman on the radio saying that she was separated. Phyllis said imagine *deliberately* saying that in public. But I liked her nerve.'

'You and Phyllis,' Moss said, not too bitterly, but the discomfort of it was getting to him. Separate simple misunderstandings and revenges were building up in them, being crammed into them from their toes up, each new row having to be pushed down on top of the last to make room for the next one. There would soon be no room for air.

'You could go and live with Dymphna again,' he said mournfully.

They were leaving each other with more grace than they'd had the day they'd got married. They were both trying hard not to want the last word.

'No, no I think I'll live on my own for a while.'

He got out of the flat without saying cheerio. It would have seemed a silly thing to say. She got back into bed to play with herself. She'd done this once before – he had been working – futtering – in the kitchen and she was supposed to be sick but in fact she just wanted to feel herself. Today she would feel herself all she liked, rub herself, pat herself, pet herself.

Rose had been in a special love with Moss in a way that she would never be again. He had taken the place of Phyllis. He had been Phyllis with sex. He had for a while believed in her. All the rest of loves would be partly for herself, she would practise saying no, and stamping her foot. She would be two and demanding again. But her husband had in the end been a mirage. Or her idea of him had been a mirage. Something had been a mirage, he wasn't there anymore. He had become love because she wanted to be loved by someone other than Phyllis, but look at him in that picture on the wall, look how he stands, holding himself two inches away from her, his fingers in a fist where it sits on her shoulder. He will not open the tight little hand and hold her properly. Getting affection out of him had indeed been like getting blood out of a turnip. He had guarded affection and affectionate words jealously, like as if there were only a few of them left. It was she who had told people how they had met – he had simply nodded assent. And made it appear no concern of his. This crude business of loving in public had been too much for him – so much too much that in the end the private was public too. Having sex became too personal. Maybe their friendship was too pure for sex – he wanted to believe that, surely time would tell that. 'If you could have taken away all the stories that we had to tell each other, or if someone else had told them cold, and if we had still loved each other, then that would have been more real.'

Rose talked it out loud to the picture.

'But love is sympathy born from lust. And I grew into the sympathy. I listened to his stories and told them to Dymphna, my heart proud, and I said wasn't that a terrible thing to happen to him or wasn't he great to be able to do that or isn't he just great. My sympathy was too much, my sympathy was born from lust and then it turned into the everyday life so convincingly that we nearly couldn't leave it because it was so much our everyday life. You cannot leave your life. But we did that, so I suppose that's something, Moss,' she whispered at him.

Rose had after all not failed. She would now find out herself about the Salem Witch Trials.

Chapter Thirteen

Rose would go to the Cliffs of Moher for the first time and there she would talk to Veronica. They would recognise places, people, she would tell Veronica how they took it. Veronica would understand.

Rose did that, made her body into a magnet and sucked consolation to herself from over an unsympathetic Atlantic. North Americans, Europeans wandered around her where she sat on the grass. They didn't interrupt. She went down the sea line further south, hitching lifts with curious inoffensive drivers. She looked over the rocks where the sea was boiling rage, making the people huddle together afraid. Rose shivered. One morning the sun shone half warm between the showers. She walked down to the sea where an early morning family were getting out of a car. The man took off his trousers, unused to not having privacy. He limped down to the sea, his two oldest sons following some yards behind him. His veins stuck out like the mountain ridges in the new expensive atlases. His stomach moved out in front of him. A large dimple in the bottom of his back, as big as Rose's fist, was the only innocent thing about him. Drizzle came down but he would swim anyway. He couldn't waste the few days holiday. The woman sat in the car with the younger children letting your father have a nice quiet swim, he must be sick of people around him all the time at work and in pubs. If only the sun would shine. She never took her eyes off that husband of hers. What on earth could she have been mourning? Whatever it was it was histories ago. The man came back, he took care that no one would see himself so, drying himself. He had become aware that he was outside. You could say that he had no need to be cautious because no one would be bothered, then again you could imagine people staring at him, at the unusual shapes of him stacked one on top of the other from his toes up. But there was no one watching except Rose and she wasn't really watching, more wondering about them to save herself wondering about herself, to save admitting that cross-roads were not always the exciting places strangers perceived them to be.

'Why am I gawking at these people's lives?'

'Because I haven't the nerve to look at my own.'

The drizzle stopped. The woman got the picnic out of the boot. She produced food, even plates, like miracles out of a small box. They surrounded her for food. The man stepped around for things like salt, sugar (none of which she'd forgotten) making sure not to bump into or touch her. In his own way Rose could see that he despised her. As for the wife . . .

Rose would have to leave them to their living. She went to eat – a white bread sandwich of Galtee cheese. There was too much milk in the tea. This would have to be her last evening. She went down to the beach again for a swim in the late day. The water was warm enough, she could smell her underarm hair. One man was walking in before her. His body was white, all the more so because of his red head. He fingered the hair on his chest wondering how he would dive. Rose twiddled her hair behind an ear. She would go in beside him, it was safer that way. They talked of the water, then swam their own ways, careful not to go too far from each other's sight. I could swim to this man and say is the bed in your B&B better than mine. This stranger. Cheerio, she called and left the water, feeling him watching her all the way to her towel. She walked slowly for him, not shy. She wrapped the towel around her and turned to catch him. He dived under and swam out. Rose grinned.

I will have to go now from this country. I have time to check the imagination. Here can make old men out of young girls. Soon I will talk of the weather and being Irish, I will sing songs and wink a lot, it will all be over before it's begun. She packed her bag satisfied, already relieved. A month later, putting her foot on the boat, she felt the relief of a person leaving a prison visit, as if she'd only had to be here because of friends. The boat, the train spinning relieved distance between her and a youth about to dry up. She could have done with a book to explain something, yet the freedom was nearly enough. Because escapes were said and thought elsewhere, they worked their way to her without her help. She loved every minute of out-the-train-window, the newness, the difference. She dropped whatever was left of how she should behave and became Rose. She would have a flittery time, she would make out of time a new youth. She would find people like herself, better still she would find people more lived-in than herself.

And this party did have lived-in people. This was where Rose wanted to be. A man who knew the man who threw the CS gas into the House of Commons, 'So he shouted, from the public gallery, you don't think its dangerous – here try this!'

'God, it must have been terrrific.'

'He was lucky too. He couldn't be done for conspiracy because he hadn't talked to anyone about it, just did it!'

You wouldn't dare say you were a pacifist, but then in the far corner of the room you wouldn't dare say anything else. Rose wouldn't. There were posters of doves beside posters of children throwing petrol bombs beside posters of children dropping roses into the mouths of guns.

'Fighting for peace is like fucking for virginity, painted right across the van in purple.'

'I liked that, much better than make love not war.'

'For war is ugly and love is lovely', a few people said in reverent litany.

'My father would have preferred me to kill someone rather than have sex.'

'My mother wouldn't have wanted me to do either.'

'Women are called birds because of the worms they pick up.'

Rose tiptoed her way several times around the room listening to them talking about themselves, their mothers, their fathers, abortion. These people were brave enough not to do things despite their mammies and daddies. The bravery took so much out of them they understood that they had to talk a lot about their mammies and daddies. Indeed they were even interested in each other's to pinpoint similarities. Her shiny brown dungarees were right, they had large pockets into which she stuffed her hands, or hand, if she was carrying another drink. That was a stroke of luck, putting on the dungarees. She could never have imagined how right they would be. The yellow bubbly blouse made up in softness what it lost in outness. Indeed she felt herself like putting one hand around her rounded breast, she wouldn't have blamed anyone else if they'd felt the same. A girl cried to another 'I know I'm supposed to believe in non-monogamy but I just get so upset when I think of him with her. I try really because it hurts Simon so much when I behave like this.'

'Maybe you should spread yourself around a little too.'

When the man asked her to his place, the man with the black polo neck and the heavy buckled belt, it had all happened very quickly, she was passing to get another drink and he'd said 'I suppose you believe in equality too.'

She stared at him. 'Women are called birds because of the worms they pick up,' Rose said, not meaning him really.

'Look, I'm only joking.'

'Of course you're joking. Men believe that women are equal so that women will do the things yous don't want to do yourselves.'

Rose was picking up confidence on her journeys round the room. She realised she'd said yous.

'Come, come, that's a little harsh.'

The conversation then calmed down somewhat, moving itself down from their head and mouths until their fingertips tingled. God, it could be Moss trying to start afresh. She could admit here that she'd already been married – liberty was so new for all of them that it would tolerate such fresh recent mistakes. But she wouldn't tell anyone. What was the point? They would dismiss it too easily. Keeping secrets was a way of life with her. It would be nearly two very long decades before the people in

152

this room would say well, you know, the children, and marriage is not such a bad thing, commitment is important.

'We could go around to my place, this party is getting too noisy.'

Rose couldn't have refused him because she would never figure out who was better than him in this room, not that she'd intended to look *for* someone but now that he was asking. Maybe he was the best, maybe it was luck. Bad luck she countenanced herself. But she would like to have a go at being promiscuous. Just once, she pleaded.

'I'll get my coat.'

Jesus, maybe it would catch up with her later somewhere later. But how Rose? You're not going to be in that sort of situation again where these things might matter. Oh I don't know I don't know, she bit her small finger nail. Still I've told him that I've just gone to get my coat, as she hauled it out from under fifty others. You wouldn't know who I'm refusing. Later is a long time away.

Rose enjoyed it like she had been waiting for this since the day she was born. If Phyllis had been told that then, life could have been different. Hers. Theirs. Twenty-one years from now what this baby will enjoy most will be a screw, sorry night, if that offends you, with someone whose name she doesn't know yet. I'm not saying that your daughter will enjoy nothing up until then or nothing better afterwards but up to that point . . . Yes indeed I do think, Mrs, that you should take that into consideration and not deny yourself too much seeing that the end result no matter what you do . . . You know the thing she will enjoy most is that she doesn't yet know his name. She will giggle about that, proudly, for years. I'm telling you . . . In the morning, 'What's your name?' She could have imagined feeling so detached. Excuse me, could you take your leg off my stomach, it's heavy, what's your name?

'Simon,' with his tongue in her mouth.

Oh God, I hope it's not her Simon.

'See you around, Rose.'

'Yes, see you, see you.'

Cheerio.

Rose went home to her new room and wrote down slogans, her head bursting out through her insides. At last, life. Where she could make a rabbit's place for herself and foray out, never to be a child of Lir again. She painted the slogans out, starting some of the words with what she knew of Celtic design. She painted them with the reverence of a day-old mother spreading out a baby to examine it.

In another month she would pack her bag for further travels, holding hands with these words, cushioned and proven right by them.

Paris, the pictures in *Stair na hEoraipe*. No one she knew around, thank God, no need to swallow. The going to places she overheard tourists talk about. The judgment of places. That was the part she liked best. Would I know the difference between a good and a bad painting? If I had been a gallery owner then, would I have said she's just like all the rest? Sitting there letting herself be painted. Give me. . . the Mona Lisa with courage. Oh God, I might have done that she thought. Better to accept what they tell me is good, this judging is tricky. I might have thrown the baby out with the bath water – still you can't leave the dirty water in the bath forever.

And how to judge the man from Amsterdam. She smoked dope with him – how hard it was to say that word. He too talked about peace, love, without insisting that she love him. Long-haired soldiers smiled at them from the newspaper headlines. How are you feeling now, is it getting to you? That embarrassed Rose. No one asked her that when she was drinking, just as well. Imagine people in a pub asking each other how the drink was affecting them. Impossibly long lanky people growing tulips to make up for ugliness. The only city for walking. She never heard the cars, the silent tread of bicycles catching up on her, passing her, voices from boats.

Rose bought a gypsy scarf and skirt and started to move eastwards. Sound and light history. She was part of history, by knowing it. She wished not to be a part of what she didn't know. She wished to classify herself. Now she was living in time, in learning, stitching pasts and presents, she was a good traveller, she didn't go soppy. She found out about places before she went to them, but she didn't believe everything she read in guide books. First she checked what they said about Ireland, if they said anything.

Rose on balance never became more important nor less important than the place she was in. She was healing up and storing up perspective for the future. She did the storing unnoticed by herself. The healing was the most important part. She found out why she couldn't spend a life with Moss. It was because it wasn't just a life, as he thought. It was hers. She found out why their love never split her insides with joy nor with ache. It was because she was not ready. He had taken the first signs of her desire and rushed it into premature shape to fit over his own needs. She decided to bury her mistake and its afterbirth. She plucked guilt out of her bloodstream, where it had been annoying her, and blew it like a feather away from the tips of her fingers.

But time with travellers, jumping their way through the unknown worlds, began to wear out. Rose felt the need to do. Do. Something to do. Do something about her own country. Let it do something for her. She had begun to develop edgy X-ray eyes, as unrested travellers must. She saw through so much it was getting hard to enjoy herself. It was getting hard to catch hold of simple unwicked things. She edged her way back to West Europe where she had to think again about Jews and Hitler and who had helped Hitler, he couldn't have done it all on his own, couldn't have put a hand over those tall very tall rickety buildings in Amsterdam to pluck out people, couldn't have found Jews in the endless maze of streets in Paris, and then she had to think of Palestine too. There was no end to it. She would welcome the uncurious days that familiarity can give.

She secured jobs serving food, cleaning toilets, to buy her fare to London, while she wrote another postcard to Phyllis. The cards had got scantier and scarcer, had become made up. If Rose could have said I did and I did and I met and I saw and I felt and I now think, but she didn't need Phyllis standing there hurt to the bone to know that half truths, cut corners, became more and more the painless method of pretence. Not saying so much opened up tracts of distance between them much bigger than the real miles. Yet Rose believed that actual nearness would solve it, would stop these wild conjecturings and accusations that she felt being heaped up against her by Phyllis. It was when writing one of these grasping attempts that the worst thing yet happened. Not the worst for Rose but the worst for Rose and Phyllis, that clinging entity which refused to give up the fight with Rose's adult life.

Rose was on the train heading for a French port where she would depart from east of Ireland – she considered England a resting spot, a relief, not geographically placed in relation to Ireland, it was too emotionally ingrown and festered to be given North South East status. She was writing the postcard and listening to noises, train noises, an engine, the shuffling of passengers, the conversations of her imagination, when she saw a man come into her carriage. Not just any man. A particular man, who burned a hole in the space between them.

Latin, she thought. Latin because she liked the sound of it, the age of it, the precision of it. He was in fact only a tanned Breton, tanned all over, he had been to a nudist colony he told Rose and she didn't even feel like blushing because train journeys – the way she became a mystery to other passengers – gave her an unwarranted amount of confidence. First she looked at him with one eighth of her right eye – the rest of her focus was on the fields. Then she had resorted to covering her face with the slightly parted fingers. She had him in there with her, the whole look of him cupped to her mouth, all of him sitting here in her palms joining her in a secret lukelit place. By the time he spoke what a world she had created out of the ordinary . . . hands, fingers, promises – no not promises – words, lips, tongues, looking, no need for even words. Addresses. We could always write. No that was too ordinary, ears, nipples. She discarded the postcard to Phyllis. Fingertips. That would be the best of all. Rose had not become a committed follower of free love, she felt that it wasn't *that* free. It was hard to explain why she suspected that someone else was writing the rules to this supposed ruleless love.

'But you can stop yourself getting pregnant now. You are as free as us.'

(Yes, stop yourself.) The answer to that might make people think she was awkward, finicky, even paranoid and Rose still wanted to be liked. But although she didn't drop like a fly into strange beds she knew that if this man had a bed, anything, even reasonableness, could be postponed.

Rose did get off the train with him. She had pulled herself up once, twice, as they exchanged conversations, giddily in the beginning. Was this not another man coming into a room worming into her imagination, batoning down sensible reserve and then when she was open, beaming, picking up his paraphernalia, saying polite goodbyes and walking to another room, she now violated for days. Was this not another . . . Was this not . . . His voice got slower as they realised that no, neither of them was going to fly out the window or move to another carriage. Her voice got deeper. She could smell him now – a slight dusty odour oozing out slowly across the carriage. Another passenger joined their conversation nervously, half in French, half in English. This was lovely – they made an outsider of him as if they were already special. They talked more and more to him in order to test out themselves as united against him. They were already lovers. They smiled across ten feet and kissed mid-air. They already felt their arms and hands and fingertips on bare skin. They wondered about the colour of their pubic hair. Hopefully they understood each other, hopefully they were not imagining things. No, there was no mistake. Until the day I die Rose said to herself I could not will not regret this. She got off the train with him.

His flat, Claude's, Claude's place, was full of his life, books photographs books tapes paints. Perhaps there were not that many things but the flat was so small it seemed to be crowded with emblems. There was a stereo, and classical records, she remembered that, Carmen playing, screaming. The flat was so small that they could barely have moved without touching each other, which they didn't want to do anyway. Rose walked from the train with him bravely. She was proud of herself for taking such a risk, in order to dispel her own reluctance she had checked again that no one was expecting her to arrive anywhere at any particular time, she said yes that of course she should use the freedom properly. No doubt it would not always be there. But when the train pulled out that was her hearth gone. She watched it briefly but Claude watched her, 'Claude ...' 'Rose...' (they laughed) and drew her into this the village where he lived and didn't lord it over her that it was she who had come to his life. They spoke little, some English less French, on the short walk to his apartment. Two surly men glowered at them over their beer cups, a bunch of teenagers slim, dark-faced, smiled encouragingly out the coffee house window.

'Glass of wine?'

'Yes, thanks.'

Rose moved her deep red glass around the plastic gingham because she feared slightly now to look at him. She peered out over the village church at fields in steps of ever-increasing green growing more certain as they reached the sky. The fields were edged or spotted with poppies. A few stray poppies crept right to the edge of the village, silent and just as daring as a black cat. But she wasn't here to think about death or war so she looked at him again. He was staring, all his admiration (he would not have trusted a strange man so much) all his desire lying bare in his eyes. He stood up and took her hand tugging her to his room, thinking that life was the loveliest of things. She ignored the train station and smiled at him.

Rose and Claude created for themselves in a small room sometimes a tornado, sometimes a quiet flame that would for the rest of their lives light up dark parts of themselves unexpectedly, like candles being lit one by one when the power goes off. They held hands, stroked, consumed and looked enough. They giggled, cried, screamed, smirked, and felt proud. There was nothing dangerous in their pride. There was something too cruel in the fact that they would part. Three days later Rose walked back to her station – this was all hers now, the whole village. Claude held her hand tightly, frightened to let her go, but she was very positive that she was on her way home. There were tears in their throats. They kissed as the same train pulled in, a long drawing in of each other into each other, the kiss piercing the light. Rose wanted to be on the train now, to be away from the sorrow of leaving him. She looked and waved and thought a perfect stranger, a total stranger, the most perfect total days that I have ever had. They held each other's addresses, he was holding her like a guarantee made of gold, diamonds, whatever is precious on this earth. Already Rose's grasp was slipping as she shivered with the terrible danger attached to such feeling. A ring is eternity because there is no beginning and no end to a circle. A person can get lost on this merry-go-round. Two sneaky clouds followed each other blacking out the sun as Rose remembered the corpse attached to love, and the train came nearer to Calais. She would try to think of him reasonably, not with such fear, but she felt already her defeat in trying to do that.

Rose had three weeks in London to think of him before she had to think of the consequences of him. She remembered bits of him, kissing each one as she did, during each day, and by the time she got home at night she had him all assembled. He even had a voice. She conversed with him, talking quite loudly, emphasising some points, laughingly letting him have his way with others – a veritable party, each night. Luckily the neighbours thought that she had company. On the twenty-second day after she had got off the train with him, she woke suddenly with a ferocious ocean of pain in her stomach. She jumped from the bed and staggered to the toilet where she retched, and retched, rested and retched. Rested, retched. And cried. Of such beginnings are we all. Rarely, if ever, does a wan characterless girl, with a face reminiscent of various fruits, faint gently for a few seconds, visit a doctor and return in the evening to a husband, blushing. Rose put her hand on her mouth, looked at herself in horror, and thought, Oh my good God, I couldn't be. (Not only could she be, she was, but that was not proven to her yet so she didn't know.) For the next week she retched so much, closed herself in so many toilets – her own, public filthy ones, pubs', friends', retching and retching. If there was anything there she'd have it up by now. By the end of the week a doctor said your test is positive and Rose, half wishing she had someone to blush to, smiled, thanked him, and went for a brandy. She knew that she would have to have this child, clear up the ghost in her, enter forever the unfinished business of creation. The brandy went down well.

She sat down when her bags were packed and thought, I will have to think Mick and Phyllis as they are now. I will have to get home soon before I'm showing, but first I must think them as they are before they know, because they'll never be the same again. The moaning will put lines on their mouths she thought, with unusual bitterness. She called them up before her and they came nearly as they were, such was how well she knew them and why.

Mick would again be looking out over the fields, contemplating the coming summer. He would have taken contentment on to himself as if it was his right, as he did at this time every year, tapping his heel on the ground, imagining how far the frost had gone in. His hearing had improved, improved all the time in fact. He sometimes thought about Rose, trying hard not to blame Phyllis when he did – well someone must be to blame – and it certainly couldn't be him. Apparently Rose was on her way home now – she'd travelled, oh she'd travelled the length and breadth of the world. She would have seen things – but in no time at all she'd be back to normal. It was good enough to be young these days – the other matter would just have to be forgotten. At least the worst was over, she couldn't do anything more than she'd already done. He would be waiting for Rose with a keener more personal but more troubled nervousness than he would wait for Veronica. This time she had better shape up. And then he tapped the ground again to stop himself from getting angry. Phyllis would be full of unbearable excitement at the thought of Rose coming home, so unbearable it made her nearly crack open, so she'd try to think of the trouble Rose had caused and when she did she thought well at least the fact that she's caused so much harm already will make her mind her step from now on. Certainly. It was too hard a thing to think of – she would concentrate on the better light in the evenings, the freshening smell. She had got used to living now with Mick, it had taken a long time. She had closed her and Mick off from Rose – to tell the truth she hadn't wanted to have to – but when Rose left what else was there to do? She would paint the front room and Rose's bedroom. From now on there would be no more trouble, no more trouble.

Chapter Fourteen

The telling was a long bad day that wouldn't end with waking up. A day which had to do exclusively with that special contradiction – menless mothers – telling them at home. Have you told them at home yet? About whatever. (Live menless mothers that is, widows are saints.) My egg is bursting out all over – maybe I could say that – or see that story about the blessed virgin well . . . no, – tact you need – see the blessed virgin well . . . It took Rose three days to get it out. There was too much kindly comfortable talk of places away, of home, of work done to the house, of things learned, she didn't want to blow it up in their faces. When she did say it she kind of tittered it out, grinning, well what much else could she do, she didn't feel like crying and the words sounded a little funny, the nerve behind the words was gone somehow in this house with the holy pictures, everything but the words was nothing, only the words mattered. And standing on their own like that without any meaning to the listeners, with a context that had nothing to do with their meaning made them sound somehow funny. But no one laughed. And Rose too withdrew from her brief minute of humour kneeling down before their venom, falling with them at their horror, weakened by the unrelentlessness of their rage. God could never have thought sex such a sin.

Rose too had difficulties thinking harmless orgasms so evil. What came out in that house for two days soiled her more than their worst ideas of sex. Rose had a working friendship with her virginity, she felt it was a continuous thing. It melted for a few days when she enjoyed another body, only when she enjoyed it, then it came back to be with her until the next time. She felt pure, ready to give and take, having a sex that was precious. Her virginity had little to do with penises – she didn't have one – her virginity was a friendly personal thing that had to do with the innocence of bodies pleasing each other. And so she was shocked to find that really they thought her a slut, how could she, how could she, how could she have. It was nothing to do with babies, it was penises going into her – that's what it was. Not even fingers – what harm could fingers do. Fingers, babies, that was not the issue – how could she, how could she. It was nothing to do either with the trouble she'd have. Nothing a man could do would ever be such a sin – murder was not even as dirty. What came out was bile. The sick of catholicism, the vomit of the religion of unmarried men, the fear of the religion of all men. The cold unforgiving hatred of warm hands roaming over warm bodies. The dread of a woman standing looking at you – steely faced but not virgin. But maybe, she tried to understand, it was the famine, it was the closing off that hunger had brought. Maybe it was too but the excuse was little use to the dirtied Rose. She left, covered in spew and blood.

The idea struck Rose when she viewed the flat. It had a half door leading from the kitchen to the hallway. Unusual for inside a house, unusual for a city. Someone must have carried it with them, pared it down, then tired of lugging memories, left it in this severe memory-silent house. The idea wouldn't go away, it dared her. So they've hurt you, they don't want to know of you and your creation, their laws are not yours, shut them out. That means closing yourself in. The half door spoke of talking to people without letting them in. The idea would not go away – make a place like a bed in the kitchen – where you can curl up, covered, and the blankets will take their lashes. Close the bottom half of the door and stay in here beside the fire.

She had never intended locking herself away for good, indeed she was never sure if she'd intended locking herself away at all. Certainly the idea had been there, so had many others, but it was the landlady who *said* that Rose had locked the bottom half of the half door and wouldn't let anyone, let her, in. She didn't know what she was doing for food but you could smell cooking once a day and if you peered in the open half of the half door you could see the shadow of Rose around the corner. If the landlady hadn't been so nosy presumably Rose would have resumed life in a week, certainly she would have – Rose was not a looper, just a once-married-now-not-married-pregnant woman – who needed to think about Ireland.

The worst part had been Whose. Oh it doesn't matter, a man I met on the train in France. Whose? What do you mean it doesn't matter – what do you mean a train? A train, they – someone – had bellowed. Perhaps the answer should not have been given if it caused such hysterics. She tried to laugh but they had heard. Claude you little beauty what trouble a sperm of yours is causing in a house hundreds of miles as the crow flies away, if a crow would fly straight across the Atlantic and the end of England and county after county to here. Funny how far a sperm can be carried. Thank God they don't fly.

The corner of the kitchen cum dining room cum sitting room cum cloakroom cum all the rooms except one, shaped into a perfect bed. It looped around the fire in order to accommodate the makeshift kitchen. She tucked a mattress into its shape, lit a crackling encouraging grate and lay down to think about it – it – that it – those things – babies growing in you, was Ireland the right place to let a baby grow in you, her own Mother – well after all – she too had grown somewhere – yes but after all it wasn't a clone that Phyllis could have expected? And after all Phyllis could have stopped Mick saying some of the things he'd said, she had been horrified yes, but felt it best to let the law of the land run its course. After all. After all.

Rose would have this out once and for all. In order to be fair, she decided to be a man, which was difficult in the circum-stances. She kept feeling pregnant, more pregnant than she'd felt up to now. OK I'll be a boy. Now a boy would be It, not the Other trying to be It. A boy would matter, could throw himself around as a teenager and could tantrum with style, people would fear him a little. A boy would become a man. But a boy wouldn't know what the Other sometimes knows, the secrets, the grandiose nature of the ordinary. She didn't like being a boy. Having a child I have opted out, she thought sadly. I've left the real world, I've given up the time that was allotted to me. Because I do not like where I see myself in that boys' world out there I will make a baby, a new world. I will pretend that things can be fixed. But of course why wouldn't I, I can have a child. It's not much I've opted out of. Perhaps this other world is the real one. Rose you fool yourself – but God it frightens them, you standing there with another bloody human inside you, ready to drop out into here, and them trying to ignore you. (Rose hadn't felt this quite yet, she wasn't big enough, yet, but she had dreamt it.) At your peril make little the talk of pressure pains, filling breasts, water gushing, shows . . . No you can't. Rose. Rose. They can. They have. But the world she'd come into, up in, insulted her. There was no place for her, her logic, her knowledge. This creating left her a way out of it.

Rose then put together a fictitious personable man with whom to fight it out. She wanted to convince him – that must mean she liked him – but he thought she was frankly off the wall lying in here letting such a little thing upset her so. Wasn't the world full of pregnant women all the time, surely they didn't all go on like this. If they did it was hard to know whether the whole thing was worth the trouble or not. But she led him with her words. She painted a picture of life and the world, her eyes on the matter illuminated shadowy parts of the whole detail and gave them as much importance as the huge parts (the important parts, he told her) of the whole picture. She had a point all right, but you couldn't ask anyone to go around examining everything all the time. Only the finicky, like her, would notice those shadowy things and after all people did have to have some relaxation. The world, the real one, was all serious. Heavens where was the fun with her, but he was drawn back to her pointing out of the shadows and that annoyed him more. He left in a hurry and met the gathering crowd at the door. He would hang around here and see how they got on with her. Rose didn't notice that he had given up and continued her conversation partly with him, partly with other fictitious voices that were griping at the door.

They overheard her murmuring, 'Excuse me you've left your footmark on my face,' and decided to get a doctor. He talked jauntily to her, in turn reassuring, then frightening Phyllis and Mick, who had arrived by now, after the landlady's telegram.

Something the matter with your daughter.

'We know there's something the matter with her,' Mick snorted but he was worried too, so they got ready. Phyllis was glad to be getting outside those four walls where his ranting and raving was getting on her nerves. Sometimes for spite she thought well so what. A man on a train is as good as any other. She thought that only for a second or two, of course.

The doctor said patiently, 'What do you mean a footmark on your face? Who has left a footmark on your face?'

Rose could have sworn that a real voice had asked her a question. She went quiet, cautiously pulling the blankets over her shoulder. The fire was still crackling – she threw coal into it every hour or so. 'Rose, I think you're taking things a little personally. I've spoken to your parents.'

'Who are you?'

'A doctor. Doctor Lysaght . . . you know.'

'Oh I see,' Rose said, knowingly.

'It's just a matter of coming to terms with these things, life, your unwanted pregnancy, indeed simply your pregnancy, your parents' natural reaction to the shock you gave them. Rose . . .'

'Whose terms? Why do we always have to come to your terms?'

Rose was up on one elbow now.

'Well, they're generally the most sensible.'

Phyllis thought he shouldn't have said that. Mick thought so as well – he knew Rose. Phyllis and Mick shifted from one foot to the other.

'You must admit they are the most sensible.'

(Jesus does he have to rub it in, Mick thought.)

'Think about it, Rose.'

'I can't think. How could I think? They won't let me think . . .

other things maybe but think! No. They wouldn't tolerate it.'

The doctor puckered his lips.

'A lot of paranoia there, I suspect.'

Phyllis said 'I don't know what you call it, but I don't know . . . I know what she *means*. I'm not saying she's right, but I know what she *means*.'

Mick bit his tongue. The temptation was there, for both of them, to scorn the other's fragility in such an unusual situation but neither fell for it. They kept an even keel with each other, glad to have someone they knew in this place, in the world indeed.

'The odd cry helps.' Phyllis ventured, but the doctor turned his body on her sharply and she thought it best to let him work it out. Presumably he must have a strategy. There was Rose again.

'It's just that they talk about Ireland. Or anywhere. Humans, or the West, or the East . . . they don't mean those places at all. They mean man in those places, Man, Man, Man. They talk about the mind, about Art, they mean Man, Man, Man. Ah!' she threw her hands up in child-like contempt, 'They think they're just It.'

Mick was annoyed. No need to go that far. He was also very worried now.

'She's gone mad altogether.'

The doctor puckered his eyebrows this time.

'No. Surprisingly there is a theory about It and the Other . . .'

He listened and thought for a while. Mick and Phyllis looked at each other, brought together again by his pronouncement, who's mad now, they thought.

'I don't want to be unreasonable of course but it's not safe. Not safe. It's an alien place out there for me and the baby.'

'Get away out of that. Look why don't you come out – if it's forgiveness you want we'll give it you. Anything but this . . .' either Phyllis or Mick roared, getting confident now, used to the oddness of standing on a landing outside a half door beside a doctor, and their daughter on the other side of the closed door. Mick was for breaking in at this stage but the doctor had some notion that it would be bad later if he did. 'I've got past the stage where forgiveness will be enough. We can forgive each other, I'll even forgive you . . .'

'*You'll* forgive *us!*' Mick screamed hysterically.

The doctor and Phyllis dragged him away from the door. Phyllis said you'll have to leave if there's one more word out of you, so he had no choice but to calm down.

'It's just I'm tired. Why do we have to fight, fight for everything here? Why is nothing ever given? Why don't they waken up some morning and give us a present? A gesture – just something we wouldn't have to fight for.'

'Who does she mean they?'

'I think she means men. Probably not *all* men but men, yes that's who she means,' the doctor said, sadly.

'All of you running around even stealing our names at night. My baby, my baby. I don't want it mixing out there. It could get a complex, at the very least. At worst it could be made into . . .'

Mick whispered to Phyllis, 'Remember that girl, that's the one she was the most friendly with ever that I knew.'

'Dymphna. Yes Dymphna – I've still got her home address.'
Send for Dymphna.

Dymphna came with great noise and a bosomy confidence. Rose heard her, 'Sure sign something's really gone wrong when you're calling on us. You must have fucked up badly if it's time to call in the women.'

Jesus, she didn't get that confidence rubbing up and down men's legs. It was a more personal, surer voice than the one Rose remembered.

'I didn't know you were home. Pregnant I believe.' Dymphna almost bayed.

'Sorry,' she nodded briefly in well-trained meaningless deference to the parents. Mick cheered up.

Dymphna had become a busy feminist, she had spoken from the back of trucks and had even been asked to represent Ireland at an international conference.

'But that's not Ireland, the Irish said, that's only women,' Dymphna bellowed in at Rose. They laughed. Mick smirked and Phyllis thought thank God. A kind of comfort came with

Dymphna, allowing nervous mirth to surface. Rose began to feel better – she should have gone to Dymphna first but who would have thought Dymphna would be like this. Rose felt embarrassed.

'Of course the landlady created this scene.'

'No, you created it yourself,' Dymphna would not let her away with pretence.

'Why not – put it down as style. We could make this part of the ritual from now on.'

Mick and Phyllis were getting impatient again. The nerve of her, chatting away there as if this was no trouble to anyone. The doctor, a well-meaning tall person felt sad again and sadder. Poor poor man.

By now they were nattering outside, reaching conclusions, stitching together answers. They were shifting their weight around on the landing, impatient to go home, like funeral goers once the coffin has gone down. Well that's that. To put them out of their misery – and to see what the weather was like – (that's what she told herself so that she could execute the walking out of this corner with some sense of normality – I must see what the day's like) – Rose shouted 'If you all go away I'll come out.'

They hurried away in case she'd change her mind.

It was a brisk cold day. Rose had never wanted to be so public, to hate so many. She felt ashamed. But even Phyllis was thinking and told her so, well you know in a country of stuffed up men, and young men going the same way, is it any wonder that a woman first pregnant in such a place would go mad for a while. Don't worry about it, you're all right now. Mick was not as content. He forgot, but in a way that set up its own demands on Rose – step one inch sideways and you'll get the cold war in the back of your neck. He put the lid on the shame of the whole thing as best he could, but he didn't manage to stamp it far down in his body. He developed no ulcer, no heart trouble, just a tendency to sore throats. Rose herself, during what she would in future call The Five Days, had put her fingers in the eyes of Ireland. She had ground them in mercilessly drawing some dubious tears. She had thumped the country in the stomach to see what would come up. And felt better of it. She didn't do this for the crack, it would have been easier not to know what she found out but at least now she knew where she stood and that had always seemed the first principle for Rose.

Phyllis thought, at five months, that Rose had got very big, very very big, all of a sudden, and sent her hot foot to the doctor in case it was twins. The novel thought of two helped really. All newses like this – slightly pelvic disproportion, positive glucose tolerance test, disappearance of heartburn, possibility of twins, disappearance of the possibility of twins, no not twins just one big healthy baby – was assistance in the cataloguing away of the first distasteful two months. Rose sometimes blurted out the silent overwhelming power she felt, big with child, size 38D bra, big stomach, baby jumping, but she usually said it to the wrong people, to women who'd not had children and who looked at her one eyebrow raised saying don't you pressurise me, or to women who'd had too many children and who snorted, Aye, power! then felt sorry for letting out such truth, or to men which was the biggest flop of all. In time she learned that it was better to stick to aches and pains, discomforts, fears, terrors and she had to admit that there were enough of them to keep conversation going for the duration of a long long gestation. The purple stretch marks, itchy now, scratched so much they bled, the recurring nightmare of babies born not looking like babies, all these minor traumas stamping her card again and again, preparing her to be a fully-fledged member of that secret haunted society – motherhood.

And what about the love? What about Claude? About three days in a French railway village surrounded by poppies, wine. About sex that no one could at first sully because they had no proof of it. About Claude, his heart thumping, her legs wrapped around his waist, as he wrote down her address. About a man who didn't know that fatherhood comes to some, deserved or not. About Claude. Simply about Claude. Rose tried to call him up, to re-draw him but what with all the trouble and then The Five Days and then the heartburn the view got dimmer. She could make up the idea of him, could be pleased for both him and her that they had known such honesty and such requited lust, could be happy that she touched his all-over tan and his heart. But the love? It couldn't stand such pressure. It had been too young to hold up against such assault. She felt it disappearing, flying away, torn screaming from her, as surely as if it was the wild swans on a winter morning. Its echo stayed a long time, its memory longer, but it came again and again to a frozen lake and had to move further away. There was nothing left but Claude, himself. Claude himself as an idea.

When the labour itself hit, Rose spent two hours thinking, suggesting, eventually insisting that there was something serious wrong with this particular one. Around midday she realised that this was indeed the normal behaviour of birth. There were not enough pain-free seconds to recover from this shock. They told her then that she had not much longer, you're doing well, five or six hours at the most. She turned her head and sank herself into a private place of war with a pain so unheard of, so impossible, so undescribed, the most secret pain in the world. It was charted ground – she had her ancestors. Would she be as silent as them, now (so as not to disturb the woman far less on than she) and in the future (so as not to disturb anyone)? Probably she would.

When it came to the last stage – you can push now Mrs, Good Girl, Push, Push, Push, Push, Good Girl you're doing great, Rose heard them and knew that this was the last stage. She would have squatted, but they weren't having any of it. Please, please. No, No, on your back is better, come on Mrs, Push. I can't any more on my back, it's cracking open. Push Mrs, and she pushed and pushed knowing in her heart that death was mostly easier than this, she pushed and cried a low moan, a midwife said you're nearly there, the head came out and the midwife cried. It was her sixth delivery. She'd cried at them all.

'You have a son' and Rose cried and cried, relief pouring out of her, shock seeping into her. She looked at him – that couldn't be hers – a boy. She knew nothing of boys – a boy, she might have to march against NATO conscription. She cried and fell asleep, big sobs punctuating light moans. She slept through the stitching of her ripped private parts, her feet hanging weakly now in the stirrups, knowing that this was easy. All these past seven months she had crossed her legs tight and prayed for forgetfulness when she thought of the stitching, prayed that the world not be as it was, prayed for the world not to be born through such a small opening, and now it was comparatively easy. She had no physical privacy left.

Afterwards they brought her tea. She sipped and named it like her ancestors and knew what it meant, 'the best cup of tea in your life'. A midwife who was a mother herself smiled conspiratorially over the rim. 'Do you the world of good, Mrs.'

When the nurses took the baby to the nursery she forgot that she had it. She couldn't forget that she had had it, but she could forget that she had it. It would take weeks to get used to, years maybe. A band of skin around her middle had grown creased and old, a fistful of space in her head would never believe what had happened. She divided in two, the part that said look at me too, I did it also, look, and then the other part that wanted to remain child or man herself, in order to claim care from other people.

The night before she left the hospital she lay awake late wondering what it would be like out there with this baby. The lights were low, nurses' feet shuffled more new mothers into rooms further up the corridor, the soft stirring of women and doll-size babies in Rose's own room was ghost-like. They had all come back from the ward of pain, each one being greeted by a sympathetic genuinely curious chorus, each one sitting up dazed to answer in stunned ritually ridiculously pleased fashion as if she was the first, 'I had a girl, I had a boy, a girl, a boy.'

Always it evened itself out. Now they were all asleep and the night outside was saying shh shh so that they could sleep more, and so that Rose could remember important things that might help to put her life back into something that she recognised. Sometimes in the last two days she had taken great comfort from making lists – an old habit to take her mind off what was really happening. Stitch cushion in sitting room, write to

Veronica, get landlord to clean chimney, apply for job, repair dripping tap, write to Claude, – at the last minute he had been scrubbed off at least thirty lists – buy baby's bath, and there the comfort left her. A baby's bath. A baby. Again this night said shh, shh, so she could remember how normal she really was, and the things that proved it, her black cord jeans, Phyllis, Mick and Phyllis streaming with laughter when they saw her baby, forgetting their grudging catholicism for the duration of the visit, her diaries, her photograph albums, souvenirs from other countries, postcards of paintings from the *Stair na hEoraipe* book, her *own* book on love and sex, those yellow zipped jeans she hadn't worn for a lifetime, oh things would be alright. She sat cross-legged on the bed, stitches already dissolving, and made a hazy plan for the next five years – one thing for each year, that should be easy enough – and looked at her son, the soft skin of him, the good looks of him – better looking than any baby she'd seen yet – the helplessness of him.

She got into the bed, her last night in a maternity hospital, and fell asleep to the shuffling sniffling noises. Tomorrow would be all right. They would manage, and some day he would spend all his excursion money on her, on some daft present, a brooch, a snowy house or map.

Epilogue

The party was a satisfied affair. Friends from Rose's various jobs, or classes, of the last few years. Patches that had lifted off the overall plan to do one thing a year. It hadn't always been that possible. At times she could have given up, have settled for a statistical definition of herself, but hardship was in the end easier for her than for most. It sharpened her wits, kept her moving during the day. When she felt herself lagging, she heard Phyllis, after some tragedy, pronounce with gratified, expected surprise 'See! She's doing far more now since . . . than she ever did before.'

Rose's guests were an inevitable mixture. There were those who had sold out, got the jobs that they claimed were important, key for 'us' to get, (US meant ME,) become part of the mechanism that keeps the days mostly popular for the majority. They still held their 'us against them' ideas which they propounded, sometimes too much, too guiltily. This was met with a thin cynicism by those who had stayed outside. But even the outside people at this party were satisfied, because by now they were assured in their methods of how to change this island, and who's with us and who is useful. Rose was sometimes during this evening and night the most satisfied of them all.

She was outside, where she had always been most comfortable. It was a good thing to have had a child. What she had done had isolated her – she'd had it too young, she'd had it in the wrong circumstances, but all those things were for the best. People spent little time talking to her as an ordinary mother so she mostly forgot that she was supposed to be just so and just so.

And yet she was. That gratified her because she felt entitled to have a child. He was five last week. This was his and her party. She had come to learn that having him had indeed been a form of escapism, but then it is gaolers who most despise escapism. The form of escapism was her valid ticket into a twilight view of mankind. She hadn't as yet begun to speak of her child always with astounded pride but sometimes she did talk of him with shy satisfaction. She had got her toilet privacy back, he no longer crawled behind her, or screamed to be let in at the bathroom door. She had left the domain of baby clothes, the lovely striped suit from Veronica, those grown up three-year old dungarees that made him look old, oh six or nine at least, that handy washable coat whose fluff always mucked up the machine. She was better for having felt pleasure when she knew his bottom was dry and not in need of Sudocream. She was the wiser for her involvement in the underground philosophies of mothers. Her curiosity had been answered. She has also won her war with Mick and Phyllis, partially. Sometimes they made her pay the price in unexpected silences, in grudging compliments thrown at the child. 'He's very good isn't he? Hmm.' 'Oh he's a great child. Really,' but mostly they pretended that her adult life, self, was not there, and they communicated with the Rose whom they had reared and still loved. Last time she was at home, they had driven past a tasteful new house.

'That's a nice house,' said Rose, meaning it.

Mick and Phyllis pulled down that mournful silence about them. Jesus, she raged what the fuck have I said now. But Mick relented, it must have been his philosophical hour.

'Smiley. Did you ever hear of that?'

'Yes. It's English, I think.'

'I see,' as if that explained it all.

'Well he came to do a job nearby, fell in with this woman and he lives with her there. Yes that's who's in that nice house.'

They kept a minute's silence for the lost world of morals, for the days when fathers could trust their daughters, for the days before the fog was lifted.

'There's a nice house too.'

'Well, that's another story.'

If there were so many stories, why then weren't they used to them by now. 'Still,' she thought, 'taking revenge, picking over the bones of other people's sins, trying to imagine them making love to someone other than their married spouse, is a national pastime.' She decided that it was time she had a party, lift herself a little after the wearing diplomacy of this weekend. Rose cheered up at the thought of it. Who would she ask? Everyone. Everyone. Ask everyone. Phyllis smiled at her, always ready to be pleased at how well Rose had done really, despite the strange routes, and isn't this a great little car. Rose smiled back, years of complicity and sympathy quickly brushing over their eyes. Then they both puckered their lips, they were remembering, they would not give an inch. It was a 'the bus fare costs six and ninepence' look from Phyllis, and Rose's was a 'leave me alone will you, you don't know everything' one. But they smiled again before night.

The large french window looked out sceptically on what passed for a growing garden. Rose always meant to make something of it. Midsummer heat surprised everyone, making them giddier than normal. Some of them needed badly to go giddy an odd time. The richer end of things was represented by Una and Dermot – there were no interesting low class politics in their house. Una respected men, without understanding them, she had his brandy ready after the evening meal – too much of it, because she knew nothing about measures, not being a drinker herself. In this one gesture she proved a fundamental something, that marriage is as important as man. In a decade they would still be together, he with an ulcer and a manageable string of affairs, she with two children and a sound marriage. So much for the See. The Saw end of this and other days were represented by Maura L who had been a prostitute. Rose had gulped when first told thinking, this is going too far, but she worried the question so much that she came out understanding better why, why, why. Maura L and Rose agreed that the clients of prostitutes were lower than the pits. Maura L had a paper headline above her bed.

'Pimping, the oldest crime in the world.'

She had given up prostitution when her child was three. Unknown to most of the partygoers there was a client in their midst – a man who had gone to a brothel. Two of the other men knew, they'd had a conversation about it one night in the pub. Bobby and J had told Shay that it would be the first place they'd go to themselves if they ever got a chance. Unknown to them Dymphna had overheard the conversation, and was holding it up her sleeve for later, today or ten years time. There were blood stains on Dymphna's brain from some of the things she knew.

Sorcha was there. She had been a beauty queen in Galway straight after she left school. One day she had to travel around the shops adorning the checkouts, so people could say: 'I saw the Miss Galway. She's not that good looking at all.' She didn't wish to be seen in the loo but eventually she had to go. A woman watched her frizzing her hair, casting her a killing look – she knew what was going on. Sorcha gathered herself as best she could to go to the next shop, the voice of the remaining occupant shouted after her when the door was open: 'Like the rest of us, Beauty Queens shit.'

'I wet myself so much laughing that I couldn't go to the next checkout, and I've never looked back since.' Sorcha smiled. A fair-haired woman was itching to get at something or someone – last week she had written a slogan on the Papal Cross – next week who knows? She found it difficult to settle herself long enough to enjoy a party. The woman beside her was wondering loudly at what age would they take her son to the men's search end of the jail. Her husband had just got sentenced. She couldn't stand the idea of the prison officers feeling her son. Her half of the room went quiet, some in embarrassment because they didn't want to have to know or think upon these unfortunate things, others because they disapproved violently of violence. They would do anything, tell lies as well, even to themselves, to wipe it out. Rose left the woman's corner hoping that this would not get out of hand. Moss was in the kitchen. Funny, she laughed to herself, she knew more than him now. Rose had met

177

him again, two years ago, walking in the street with a new wife. He had got an English address, got an English divorce and married another Irish woman. She was in the kitchen now, prompting Moss, encouraging him in this company. Sometimes she encouraged him too quickly – a sort of go on hurry up explain to them what you mean the thing you told me, tone of voice. Lilian was her name. Lilian had been in the same night class as Rose – always sat at the other end of the room. Lilian wore expensive fitted dresses, silk scarves and jewellery. When Moss introduced her, that day on the street, Rose had thought, ah another reformed drop-out. After that, at the end of class, she had tea with Lilian sometimes. They talked about pale limp things, never about women, themselves or men. They still sat at opposite ends of the classroom. Lilian asked her now how the idea for the travel book was coming on. Fine, Rose said, fine, we've found out about some interesting epic journeys by women.

'Really,' Moss and Lilian said together.

Yes really Rose said to herself and I might just do it. Moss was turning into a type. He would go to the shop all right but only in the car because he would not carry a shopping bag. Last year his wife had had to say, 'Doctor he's got a lump, and you know what it's like, he won't come himself.' She then had to sit mortified through the expected and the only possible answer, 'Well I'm afraid he'll have to come, you're not much use' but that was last year. Lilian sometimes wished he wasn't such an old man. Still all was well – yet she had a private worry, his manners could be better, she hadn't noticed the first year, she was too busy listening to him. Still all was well.

Rose said hello to Dan. His wife was in the bedroom changing the baby. Because he had shown such a dazzled interest, beyond the call of duty, in the technical end of the Caesarean Section he felt that he had done his bit. Still all was well.

'One of those women only meetings, now what I call them is . . .' Rose had got rid of the word Only. She said All Women. No Only. She'd turned it around on her tongue, then said it out loud to herself to see what it sounded like and it was right. That was

Dan, wasn't it? complaining. Don't worry Dan all is well. Rose had become temporarily impatient.

The party filtered through the night, people dropping out when the fancy took them or when someone had rubbed them up the wrong way and they wanted to get home to their own fires. After midnight, tipsy people, some strangers, dropped in, casual as to whether they'd been asked or not. The talk rose pleasantly, the music smooched like liquid through this recently created shelter. Nothing could harm anyone here now, they could have been in a dark smoky beer cellar for all the world could get near them. One of the late comers, Eugene, was being kind to Rose in an interested fashion, turning his head to look at her, trying to elicit conversation from her. He straightened his shoulders in a private movement, trying to establish for himself that he had a right to look at her invitingly. But for the moment she was feeling a heat of her own.

An afterglow had descended on her. The afterglow of three days spent in France with a man called Claude, oh this man called Claude. Anytime she tried to recall it, it eluded her but here it was now unbidden and all the more welcome for that surprise. The six years between them now – years of mostly passionless hours – did not exist. She chose now – no not just chose – she *could* now remember his body and not just remember what it looked like. Brown soft skin made for sand and walking confidently, curly pubic hair edging its way up in scattered tufts to his chest, a deep hollow at the bottom of his back – so deep she could have rested her head there. And what she had thought when she looked at him. About the outside world and how it was for her a 'notion' of freedom, only a notion. And how she had *seen* him, more truly than he saw himself, but that wasn't arrogance on her part, it was just sadness. (In fact, Rose thought he was the one who deserved to have confidence but he chose not to know it, another pleasant trait.) Her sadness came from the desperate distance between how truly young and inexperienced she was and yet how truly old she was, because of some of the responsibilities she took upon herself, for the way things are and also for Phyllis. And then she had looked at his body again and his face, thinking what a privilege. She had got off the bed with no clothes on and sat on the floor with her back straight against the wall and he said 'How bold you are.' She had thought: 'Me?', then smiled at him gratefully because he meant it and she knew without knowing that this truthful unself-conscious sentence would sometime in the blackest moments of the future make her say I am, I am all right. What wouldn't it be like to have him stand in this room just now as if the years had never been, which they mostly hadn't. Rose sighed.

She had written to him, three years ago, just to test the ground. Claude had written back. 'Do come to the house. My wife knows.' Knows what, she had laughed to herself and then narrowed her eyes, 'I did not of course know about the child, how could I, but I've told my wife now and it is all right also.'

But no, Rose did not want to meet his wife, she did not want to be roped into a sophisticated acceptance. But next year she would go to meet him. Next year. Perhaps she should now think of some other man. Right now. That man there who was looking at her. Perhaps. He certainly wouldn't be able to parcel her off in his head as someone looking for a husband, or a child. She'd had both. And after them she had gone out to meet a world that others usually left in order to marry. Yes, that man there – perhaps. Love could sometimes be disgusting it its own way – such unbecoming dependence, but love, like sex, would hunt away thoughts of death, and might bring stars with it.

No matter what happened now Rose was versed in the necessity of finding out what there was to know. Better still she had found the index box. The sad fact might be that what she found out had already been known and buried, by one of her own women dead in the famine, or married, name lost, in Dagenham, or stuck in Chicago rearing wealthy, uppity children she didn't understand, or mourning secretly the loss of a grandmother's sister sold to a North American, catholic family. The glad thing was that Rose had the index box.

The daily news, in itself, was not always important now to Rose. It had often to be left behind in the grander search for some sort of woman's truth that could be stitched together with what was already there to make a whole truth. The search was always hampered by the terrible forgetting that had been done – the finger-work, the words, the thoughts of dead women. Often the weighty tons of forgotten words threatened to crush her. But then she had done her own useful forgetting. She didn't, for instance, remember that God would get her in the end. The fact that every Sabbath millions of grown men put their hands out and commanded people to listen to only them, meant that there was a slight danger either that she would remember or explode. But for the moment she had forgotten.

Rose's own important pleasures were those two poems she'd found last week and the fact that she now knew the woman who had painted the Papal Cross. She understood more than politics of oppression. Her senses of injustice were not just about power – who had it when she hadn't – they were also about people, herself and those she didn't know. She didn't always want to give herself up for scrutiny, sometimes she liked to float unseen, but yesterday she had begun to prepare for something new. She had pinned scraps of her past and a few desires for the future on to a mirror, making them look at each other like letters in an alphabet. She had turned on the light and let herself stand in the glare. And still her pleasures included memories of winter swans and still most of all spring days.